APHRODITE OVERBOARD

The Erotic Memoirs of a Victorian Lady

R V Raiment

velluminous

Published by Velluminous Press
www.velluminous.com

Copyright © R V Raiment 2006
www.vraimenterotique.com

The Author asserts the moral right to be
identified as the author of this work.

ISBN-13: 978-1-905605-04-0
ISBN-10: 1-905605-04-8

APHRODITE
OVERBOARD

For Jean, Christopher and my Jenny

A Manuscript Discovered

The manuscript, handwritten on stained and yellowed parchment, had been compressed for some two hundred years near the bottom of the ancient, battered sea-chest in which I'd found it. Left to me as part of my mother's bequest only after its having mouldered in the attics of several generations of her family, the document had, upon discovery, to be teased apart, brittle and tending to crumble. I am glad, however, that I made the effort, astounded by my discovery, and thrilled to see the beautiful, carefully rounded hand in which the words of Great, Great, Grandmamma are formed.

I was aware already that my Great Grandfather had exotic tropic island connections, but the manner in which they came about has always seemed something of a secret, and not to be talked about. Now, perhaps, I understand why.

I have checked what can be checked of my great, great grandmother's history and of my great grandfather's, her son. I have found, in the process, family records of her voyage and her disappearance, and official records of the loss of the 'Talisman', her crew and passengers—including a certain Alfred Smythe—at sea. There remains in question only that which cannot be proved, those matters to which only Smythe, Great, Great, Grandmamma and some others lost to history were witness.

Is this, then, her history? Or is it perhaps but the extraordinary invention of an extraordinary woman, alive through the days of Nelson, Wellington, Bonaparte and the young Victoria Regina? You must, of course, decide that for yourself…

Aphrodite Overboard
The Personal Memoirs of Susanna, Lady F.

I begin, knowing that what I write may never be read, knowing that law and the possibility of scandal may erase forever my name and account for fear of offending that most strange idea, that thing they call 'public decency'. I must observe that in matters sexual I have noticed but little in the public of decency, for whom smut and innuendo seem so often the very stuff of life, yet, because that which I write cannot be expressed in inexplicit language, I know it may be more than public morals can bear.

I hope that this may be read one day and, should it be so, I hope, above all, that it is understood.

Chapter the First

*In which I encounter an ugly little ship and an ugly little man
and in which they come to grief.*

I cannot say that the prospect of the voyage on the Talisman
endowed me with much excitement. Lord F, my husband,
promoted to early governance of one of His Majesty's smaller island possessions, had sent for me as he had threatened. In
consequence I was about to be plucked from the cosmopolitan
and exciting whirl of fashionable London in which, to be fair, I
had begun to enjoy making the most of my own particular assets
and the freedom of being an effectual widow.

Those assets, it may be appropriate to record, included a
body barely twenty-one years of age and of comely proportions
very appropriate to the latest fashions come from France. The
French Empress, I know, was not at a height of popularity in her
own country at that moment and, indeed, one wondered where
such vociferous hatred of a monarchy might end. That it was to
end for her so brutally was then beyond the imagination of any
English Lady.

One must acknowledge an indebtedness to her, though, for
the mode then current which had allowed some of us to abandon
the lately fashionable preposterous wigs, to present the glory of
our bubbies almost to their little pink noses in glorious décolle-
tage, and to tantalise our men-folk in gowns which draped from
the gatherings beneath our bosoms and floated and clung in tantalising, almost transparent gauziness. Some, I know, had taken
to wearing pink body-stockings which hugged their figure and
were implicit of nakedness beneath their robes, but I preferred
the reality. And, indeed, so did my gentlemen.

Lord F, in truth, my husband of but few months, I had found
to be not the best endowed of men, either in his wit, his intelligence, simple gentlemanliness or, indeed, his manhood. His private manners were rather rough and coarse, and what hung — if

hung is the word—betwixt his legs was rather a fair reflection of the man to whom it belonged—rather wizened, pale, short of stature and somewhat insubstantial.

No virgin when I met him, I had encountered other men, including one joyously rounded youth who worked in my father's stables, whose yard of flesh had in repose promised of nothing substantial and yet, upon excitement, proved prodigious. Not so Lord F, who never did other than briefly impale me upon his short pink prod before gasping and floundering with an excitement of coming which I found quite incomprehensible.

Our honeymoon period lasting in proportion perhaps to his virility, he was soon dipping his slender wick in cunnies other than my own, and in women bought or trading themselves in hope of some preferment. And left much to my own devices I had little hardship in finding myself some gentlemen whose own little 'gentlemen' were of a more robust and fulfilling nature, and I took much pleasure in them. But it was not to last.

The Talisman was a shabby little craft, crewed by shabby little men and protected by the merest handful of little guns. Whilst other craft relied upon great arsenals to protect them, others upon fewer guns but a wicked turn of speed, I do believe the Talisman relied upon its visual inconsequence. Indeed the grubby little vessel appeared to have made itself a floating nonentity so inconsiderable on any mark that no enemy would demean himself by deigning to attack it.

What she carried in her bowels I never sought to establish and neither do I care now. I remember only the awful rolling motion of her, the incessant noise of wind and creaking timbers, squealing braces, shouted orders and the thunder of running feet upon the deck. I remember the awareness of our lack of privacy in the cupboard of a cabin I was forced to share with my maid. Having walls of knot-holed planks on three sides and a sheet of sail canvas upon the fourth, one was constantly aware of being overlooked by lecherous eyes, overheard by coarsely lecherous ears.

And Alfred Smythe had eyes and ears for all, a man whose

obsequious essays in surface manners could not diminish the sense that one always stood before him naked and under coarse appraisal. I felt for him an instant loathing and feel it still, regardless that he saved my life.

He was, it seems, an island trader of some sort, and stowed upon the foredeck of the ship was a longboat of his own, covered in tarpaulin and bulking with stored goods in which he made his trade. Being but one of two women on board the ship, and frequently abandoned by the other, my maid, a lusty little soul who doubtless spent a large part of the voyage with her legs spread somewhere in the tweendecks, I was often hungry for company.

My appointed escort was a certain lieutenant Trubshawe, whose father had no doubt purchased the lieutenant's commission in order to rid himself of a grievous irritation and who, in doing so, proved much more efficacious than he ever might have guessed. A vacuous individual of porcine build and expression, Trubshawe was one of those men who knows no business of his own yet considers himself an authority upon everyone else's . From the instant of our departure, it seemed to me, he began to lecture everyone, from the captain to the cabin-boy, on the correct manner in which to pursue everything from navigating the ship to tying a sailor's knot.

Needless to say, this did not make the Lieutenant any more popular with the crew than he was with me. I suppose I resented the suggestion that I needed an escort of any kind, other than my attendant maid, and the poor fellow had that resentment to endure as well as whatever other insecurities rendered him such an oaf. In my regard, too, he seemed to have somewhat of a hair trigger, so that within a few seconds of being in my presence the front of his breeches came rather to resemble a military campaign tent and, flushed and embarrassed, he needed to make himself quite rapidly absent.

So lonely was I at times, though, that I bitterly regretted his ineffectuality as a companion and conversationalist. The only other male passenger, the crew being perpetually occupied with keeping our ugly little craft afloat and on course, was Smythe,

the trader. Though an odious—and malodorous—little man, the journey proved to be so interminable and so interminably tedious and boring, and the ship so small, precluding easy escape from anyone's company, that I found myself one hot and sunny day being treated by Smythe to an inventory of his small boat's manifest.

"Guns, milady," he announced. He'd removed the tarpaulin for a while to dry out any moisture which might have seeped under it, displaying the mound of casks, kegs, boxes and suchlike containers which housed his supplies and trade, and was tapping a long wooden case with a rattan cane.

"Have to have guns, milady. There's lots of folks settled upon the main and nearer islands who needs to think of their own protection, and I likes to have a few extra to hand meself, too."

"Is it really so dangerous, then?" I will admit that this detail was of interest to me since I was about to take up residence in what I had heard described as an island paradise, a veritable Eden on Earth, and could not for the life of me recollect either Adam or Eve demonstrating any requirement for firearms in their history.

"It can be, milady. Of course, where you'll be, in the Governor's palace, you'll not find much as needs to be shot at, but about the islands generally white folks do tend to stand in need of some protection."

"You mean from lions, tigers, that sort of thing?"

The little man smiled, or rather leered, and affected an insolently patronising tone:

"Lord no, milady. There's nivver such a thing as big cats or bears or anything like them on the islands, and what beasts there are, are precious small in the main. But some of the people are, well, a little dangerous."

"The islanders? According to my husband they regard we white Europeans as little less than gods."

"'Tain't just the islanders, ma'am! The days of Blackbeard and Captain Kidd may be long gone, but there're still some bold piratical types about, and you never know when the bloody French'll come spoiling for a fight. As fer regarding white folks as gods, well 'tis true of some of the islanders," he answered smiling, "but not of all.

"There's some as are not entirely grateful for Britannia's enlightenment. There's some, it seems, don't like the importation of our religion one bit, and there's even more can't seem to fit themselves to the idea of regular labour. The colony's been importing blacks fer years, of course, to work the plantations, solely on account of the resident fuzzies being the laziest buggers in God's Creation. And some of 'em have even started blaming us for the maladies that abound among their villages, blaming the poxes of their filth and ignorance upon our own Jack Tars, God bless 'em."

"I see," I said. The imperfect vision of paradise rendered by my husband's somewhat tedious and uninspired penmanship and the glowing vision others, more poetic, had suggested to me, seemed suddenly very unconvincing. I better understood the politely sympathetic responses of certain older ladies of my acquaintance to the news of my departure.

"And this here's whiskey," he said, tapping a pile of kegs. "Lots of the fuzzies like a tot or two, but the buggers are inclined to pinch it, if you let 'em."

"And these?" I was pointing at some small bales which looked familiar.

"Fabrics, milady; bright colours, bright patterns for the fuzzy ladies." Smythe winked at me—perhaps the most lascivious wink I have ever encountered.

"Time was," he said, "when I first come out here, that the fuzzies' ladies paraded round mostly starkers. There were little brown bubbies everywhere, lovely little round arses and, twixt the nethers of some, scarcely more than a piece of string." He sighed. "Now, of course, what with the presence of the church and with desiring to abate the interest of our jolly tars, the lovely ladies cover up. A bitter disappointment, is that, for some of us."

"You forget yourself, Mr Smythe," I chided him firmly: "You

forget, moreover, to whom you are speaking."

Smythe only smiled and I turned brusquely away, not deigning to respond to the fact that his gnarled right hand now rested, gently kneading, on his crotch.

I didn't see the inside of that boat again until the night of the storm, that seemingly interminable nightmare of shrieking, howling wind and a sea that roared and pounded in its infinite anger till it thrust us upon the reef. I remember the ship striking, the sudden shuddering vibration of everything around me, the scream of tortured, grinding timbers and the shouts of terror and alarm.

I remembered nothing more, till I woke up in the boat.

The baggage in the boat—all of which seemed to have been kept sound—did not conspire to make it comfortable. Hard edges seemed to dig everywhere into my aching, weary bones and scored my flesh as my body slid with the motion of the craft. Smythe was at the tiller; the small sail raised, and saw me wake. He did not wait for me to speak.

"S'just you and me, now, my lady," he said: "All the others is gone—gone to the bottom and to Davy Jones's locker. Part o' the main mast toppled onto the ship's boat and stove her in, crushed the few that were in it. Folks was swept overboard as fast as they came on deck. I found you out cold in your cabin, brung you to my boat and tethered you aboard. Fortunately the old Talisman settled slowly by the bows and, in the end, all I needed to do was wait for the water to reach our keel and carry us away.

"'Course a few silly sods tried to join us," he smiled cruelly; "but she's all the weight that she can carry, so I discouraged them." So saying, he tapped the butt of a pistol in his belt. "She's my boat," he added, as if that resolved the matter.

I don't know if it was the matter-of-fact way in which he addressed it, whether it was that I had lost little aboard the ship that was actually irreplaceable, or whether it was finding myself safely—as I thought—aboard the well-provisioned, long, slim boat, but I did not descend immediately into the terror of despair I could so easily have imagined. Even the natural grief that must come to me over the loss of poor little Esme—my maid—was forced into abeyance as I addressed him:

"Remembering the fury of the storm, Mr Smythe, and our impacting upon whatever obstacle it was that sank us, I must express my profound gratitude that you should have undertaken such a risk at such a dangerous time in order to bear me safely away. And in that regard and in such circumstances, I entirely understand, and warmly congratulate you, upon the caution, Mr Smythe, which caused you to bind me to your craft to keep me safe amid the storm. I do not quite understand why it is that I remain thus tethered now?"

For tethered I was. My wrists roped together above my head were tied, it transpired, to a stubby little bowsprit, a timber post projecting over the prow, or front, of the craft. Each of my ankles was separately bound by lengths of rope to what I know are called the rowlocks, horseshoe-shaped metal projections either side of the boat in which, when used, the oars are gripped.

My gown—the same I wore that awful night—appeared to have blown up around my bosom and, in the fullness of both, imposed a limit upon my view. But I could feel, quite distinctly, that the heavy drawers which no lady of fashion wore at that time but which I had caused Esme to make to safeguard my modesty on the voyage, were not at all in evidence. I remembered, distinctly, wearing them the night that the Talisman foundered and was somewhat perplexed at their absence.

Unaccustomed to either unfettered sun or sea-breeze my cunny tingled warmly to the caress of both and, indeed, to the unobstructed and quite unwavering gaze of a grinning Alfred Smythe.

"What, quite, do you mean by this?" I asked him. Smythe only smiled, and it was not a smile I liked, then he tut-tutted, as if experiencing some regret.

"Poor lady," he said. "Truth is, you see, I took something of a shine to you when you first come aboard the Talisman, and all these long weeks' journey have been so much longer on account of knowing that you would never've let me near you. I know, of course, that you despise me as a lady of your station must, and I'm not, of course, surprised. But I couldn't help wanting you, you see. You're a lovely, luscious lady, milady, and peeping at you from time to time through a knothole in your cabin wall I've glimpsed that lovely round pink arse, the glory of those dumplings. So many sleepless nights, milady, my own hand round my plunger, wishing it were your'n, and jacking off into my kerchief my only consolation.

"Only now you're mine, you see. The Talisman's gone down, with all hands, and for all the world can know you've gone down with her. No bugger's gonna come lookin' for you, and here you are, with me—and mine."

I can't say that I thought his words endearing, but I'm not a fool. Lost upon sea-lanes ill-frequented by civilised ships and as likely to be found by seafaring bandits as saviours, I knew I was in a poor way to defend myself or what would quaintly be called my honour. For it's not as if my 'honour' has not been dipped into by odious little men before, at my behest or my husband's.

"Will it please you then," I asked him as if surprised; "to take me thus—unwilling?"

"'Twill please me, my lady, to take you any way I can," he answered firmly.

I smiled at him with all the practised condescension I could muster:

"I can see, Alfred, that there's little I can do to prevent you doing as you will and taking pleasure in it, though I have to warn you that, should you leave me thus, I shall do all that little that I can." I could see my tone affected him, the smile going out of his eyes.

"I'm not a virgin, Alfred." I told him smiling: "I've been taken thus—roped and bound—before for another man's pleasure or for mine own, but I'll not be taken thus without consent and give you aught to find joy in."

"What yer sayin'?" he demanded, sullenly perplexed.

"Poor Alfred! You look upon me and you want me. I understand that. I am quite at ease with that. You are not, by any means, the first. But if you take me as I am, then what? You'll insert your cock within me, find me dry. And I shall lie back and think of other things, render myself inert, and make you a gift of my body as a handsome, lifeless mattress. Perhaps you want me to fight you? I will not. Perhaps you want me to pretend to enjoy you? I will not. You will do as you wish to do, empty your need into me, and probably derive less pleasure than you would were I but your 'kerchief."

I could see he was disturbed, either by my threatened passivity or by my manner, startled no doubt by my nonchalance and soft disdain.

"You'll fight me if I hurt you enough!" he hissed.

"You really think so, Alfred? I find it hard to believe that someone of your station has not observed what hard and callous bastards are the nobility of our nation. D'you really believe the arse you find so desirable has not been paddled vicious hard—and striped—by some of their lusting lordships? D'you fancy there's a fragment of this pinkly bolstered body that's not been smote or bitten to excess?"

His expression had grown dark and sulky, that of a spoiled child fearing to be deprived of a promised sweetmeat:

"If 'tis the only way I can have you, 'twill suffice!"

"Foolish man!" I chided him: "Why should it be the only way?"

"Whaddyer mean?"

"I've already made it clear to you, poor Alfred, that I'm a woman who takes pleasure in men—even sometimes men who behave roughly. Now all this talk of fucking—though we've never used the word—has already begun to tell on me, and you seem to forget that all these weeks I've been closeted aboard that awful little ship without a single todger to take pleasure in. I am hungry for a man, Alfred, and not only could that man be you but really, if we are honest, it should be you. Have you not saved my life? Untie me, you silly boy, and come to me my hero, not my villain!"

"The time ain't right."

"Your pardon?"

"I needs to stay where I am, at the tiller, mindin' the sail. The wind can change in an instant, and there's a haze out there that could be land. I needs to keep my eyes and hands a-ready."

I nodded, assuming an expression of one bowing to superior wisdom—a skill all ladies must acquire:

"I can see you have skilful hands, Alfred. I do admire skilful hands."

Ignoring that, he said:

"'Tis land I see, and an hour or two should bring us to it."

"What land, d'you think?" I asked him, secretly quite excited.

"Dunno," he answered flatly; "could be almost anywhere."

I smiled inside:

"Then should you not untie me anyway? Suppose we land and find Authority?"

Great caution suddenly appeared in his eyes. He knew, of course, that should we land anywhere under European control my word and the tether marks upon my wrists and ankles could see him dead within hours.

"Maybe I'd better drop you overboard," he responded with chilling matter-of-factness. "I've seen plenty of shark fins about — they'd not leave you threshing for long."

I had perforce to work very hard, at that moment, at keeping my voice soft and level. Except for the one time a mariner fishing had brought one of the monsters up on deck I had never seen a shark, save as a shadow in the water, but what I'd glimpsed the once and all I had subsequently heard had given me an exquisite terror of them. Never will I forget that creature, huge and threshing in its death throes, steel grey as a sky full of threatening storm, eyes of a ghost, its mouth gaping and grinning—it seemed to me—with an evil lust for murder.

Though terrified, I responded quickly:

"Maybe you had better," I answered as levelly as I could; "though I would have thought you'd prefer a happier ending."

"What're you talking about?"

"Alfred, dear; haven't you understood anything yet? So far as I am concerned you are my hero. All the while we were talking I could see your own little hero pressing forward against your breeches and, free, I should be happy to console him. Moreover, should we land safely among our own kind I can promise you not only some of the most delightful fucking you have ever known but I shall make your name a hero's name, so long as you set me free. You can have me, if you want me, fame as well, and a handsome reward from my cuckold husband for good measure."

"And if the island's deserted?" I heard a catch, eloquent of lust, in his grating voice.

"Then you will have me still, a willing concubine and lover, taking care of you and looking to you for protection!"

I could see him melting. I struck my last blow:

"Dump me over the side and, if the land ahead is deserted, what have you gained? Set me free and I am yours in any and every way you might desire. My mouth, my bubbies, my cunny—even my arse, should that please you—are willingly yours. Indeed, free me now and I shall give you a pleasure such as you may only yet have dreamed of."

"What pleasure?"

"Set me free, Alfred, and ere the boat comes in hail of land I shall pleasure you most sweetly."

"Can't," he said: "Told you. Need my eyes and hands."

"And you may keep them both, Alfred. You've gazed too long on my cunny, Alfred, and given not enough thought to my other lips. Can you not imagine how you would feel to sail your boat to the shore, a noble lady and governor's wife upon her knees before you with your cock inside her warm wet mouth, your juices slithering within her long, pale neck?"

Rarely have I seen a man move so swiftly, tethering the tiller in place with a rope, striding across the deck and slicing the binding ropes apart in four simple strokes of his rather large knife. Then he was back in his seat, and bulging.

I stood up as best I dared, stretched my aching limbs, then tottered and half fell, half crawled toward him. Just as I had promised I lowered myself onto my knees before him, unfastened the cock-flap of his breeches and lowered it.

In fairness to the man I should report that that which sprang forward was a joy to behold, all purple-headed, hard and corded, dribbling a little of his milky promise. I said: "What a lovely little fellow, Alfred, and really not so very little, either!" and, knowing what must be done I bowed and tongued it, not without a modicum of pleasure, enjoying—as always—that unique, strange taste and texture, and then engulfed him, heard him gasp and moan, felt his arse squirm upon the wooden seat.

I must wonder at the steadiness of the course he steered for those long moments, for I have some expertise in fellatio's noble art, and as I slid, and stroked, and plunged, licking and flicking, nibbling and suckling, poor Alfred became quite hysterically mobile. It suited me. It suited me to please him and to please myself, for who could know—should the land ahead prove deserted—how long it might be ere I would know the fullness and taste of a manhood again?

"Oh my lovely, lovely lady!" he cried, shuddering with passion as he came; "Never have I dreamed…" and then I shot him.

He'd been sitting all the while, you see, with the cocked long pistol in his waist-belt. His hands on the tiller, eyes closed in exultation as my mouth moved on his swollen, hungry member—I doubt he even felt me take the pistol, lift and fire it.

I smelled burnt hair and hoped it was not my own fair tresses, and I saw his staring, disbelieving eyes. The wound was large, quickly seeping a deal of blood, but whilst I had rendered him seriously indisposed I had not killed him. For that I was quite glad, for his presumption and his viciousness had angered me greatly. I, smiling, took hold of his unresisting feet, lifted them abruptly and tipped him easily backwards and into the great blue ocean. And I must surmise he told me the truth about seeing sharks, for poor Alfred did not thresh long, and the last I knew of him was a gurgling cry of terror.

I had, in truth, been rather brave in disposing of my pilot, for I was not at all certain of my handling of a boat, but he had set it well, the sail carried me forward without straining, and the tiller quickly felt familiar to my grasp. Within an hour, perhaps, the little boat's keel grated on sand and I was able to step out, free, onto a beautiful sunlit—and deserted—beach.

Chapter the Second

*In which I encounter Paradise,
and a most remarkable form of welcome.*

Despite frequent temptation, I had never actually murdered a man before in other than my heart. The reality, coupled with the exertion, no doubt, of bringing my small craft to shore—a feat which seemed to have extracted from me more energy than I first surmised—produced a sudden and powerful reaction. Overwhelmed, I sat for a while upon the sand, my head reposing between my knees, feeling exceedingly sick and faint.

That nausea and weariness soon passing, however, I then arose and gazed about me. My swift-reviving senses perceived an infinity of empty golden sand, the sea it's one margin, dense forest and undergrowth it's other, and brought to my ears the distant cry and chatter of forest birds as yet invisible to me in the dense greenery.

After my narrow escape from Smythe's clutches and weeks of confinement within the small, too-crowded ship, the warmth and quietude were a balm to me. Even the thought that I might be alone here did not, at first, too much disquiet me.

There could, of course, be people here, despite that the whole place somehow felt as if it might never have known a human's tread before and, rather foolishly perhaps—given Smythe's warning about the antipathy of certain islanders—I proceeded to stride about the beach for a while, hallooing, lest anyone might hear me and come to my aid. No one did.

Upon reflection, now, it rather astounds me that I was not then more circumspect. There was I, a woman alone, the weapons available to my immediate defence consisting of my own modest physical strength and a single, discharged pistol for which I had not even ventured to seek fresh powder and shot. Smythe himself, in earlier conversations had intimated very clearly that not all native populations in the area were friendly, and had dwelt in rather greater detail than would any man of taste upon the allegedly cannibalistic tendencies of some.

Alone, then, and to all intents and purposes unarmed, I stood upon a foreign—nay, an alien—shore, within secret sight, for aught I knew, of man or beast to whom I might represent nothing more than an item on the bill of fare, and yet I felt somehow miraculously safe and at peace!

For as long as I could remember I had always found an untoward joy in seclusion, perhaps from having been raised in a large house always full of servants, the indentured children of servants, farmers, horse-traders, seed merchants and their various agents. And thereafter, of course, life in my husband's house and particularly in the social throng of London remained ever hectic, and it was always difficult for me to find an opportunity to be alone, to reflect in solitude. Now I seemed to have it in abundance.

Never had I felt such a glorious sense of being alone, as I stood, bathed in sunshine amid a paradise of gold and blue and green. And this wondrous feeling, together with the continued absence of response to my first hallooing, emboldened me to do something I would never otherwise have considered. Giggling and happy as a schoolgirl in the sun I shed my clothes entire, the better to wash them in the sea, to bathe and revive myself.

Naked still, the sun warm on my shoulders and haunches, a soft sea breeze but kissing every piquant extremity of me, I began to strive to drag the longboat up and out of the water, confident that the supplies within would help me toward salvation. But in the shallows, barely out of the water the laden boat was heavy, ungainly and stubborn as sin, and I struggled against all hope.

Only then brown arms appeared, brown hands appended, and a number of brown bodies, at which I scarcely dared to look, took hold of the vessel with me and drew it easily across the sand.

My sudden collaborators comprised about a dozen men, and they could hardly have appeared more frightening even though their first action had been to aid me. Never, ever, did an English-woman of rank and fashion encounter such assistance!

Naked as new-born babies they were, for the most part, though there was nothing baby-like about their too-obvious en-dowments. All had bodies near as perfect as those of athletic boys despite the fact that several were clearly of some age, their faces seamed and wrinkled, hair greying to the sides and temples. Some were boys though, or at least young men, and every one was armed, moreover. Among them I saw spears with wicked-looking points, whilst one or two carried hefty clubs and oth-ers, more astonishingly, carried swords. Most remarkably these broad, flat-bladed weapons, intricately engraved, were fashioned not of bronze or steel but from a wood of stygian blackness.

All the men wore paint upon their bodies—and indeed upon all parts of their bodies—in spots and stripes and zigzags of white, black, red and yellow. A number wore feathers and animal quills (like those of a hedgehog but longer) in their hair, together with bracelets and necklaces of beads, stones and pieces of bone. But there was not a loin-cloth nor a set of drawers among them, their pizzles hanging long, lean, somewhat pointy, and, save where painted, deliciously brown.

Making my swift appraisal of them, I noted that that curly black hair which had earned so many of their kind the title 'fuzzy-wuzzie' was here to be found only nestling around their balls. Their head hair was long and straight and plaited in intri-cate ropes and coils, and I was particularly taken with the large appearance of their dark, moist eyes and the girlish long lashes with which most were graced.

So caught up was I in my reverie, tinged with no little appre-hension as to what now might befall me, that I scarcely noticed at first their own rather studied appraisal of my self. And it sud-denly struck me with loins-churning force that I was more naked than they were.

What brought me most resoundingly to that remembrance was when one of the men—a tall, young, handsome fellow with the carriage of authority—reached gently, even reverentially, toward me and touched the curls of golden hair which now hung untrammelled about my shoulders. I am, of course, quite fair, and it was clearly this, as much as anything else, which astounded them. Now—freakishly, I am assured—nature has blessed me with fair hair upon my mound as well, and, seemingly naturally and without any sense of impertinence, the authoritative young man reached out and touched this too. As he did so, and rather to my surprise, he and the whole half-encircling assembly moaned softly aloud with an intensity the like of which I've never heard, save when I've been mouth-milking some lucky fellow's yard.

It was at this point that they knelt, all but one, in the sand, before me, collapsing to their knees almost simultaneously. Only one, an older fellow with a quite ferocious visage and wearing an animal quill—hard as it is to credit, through a fold of skin at the base of his member—remained rather self-consciously standing. An undeniably pointed look from the young apparent-leader, however, brought the older man somewhat sulkily and reluctantly to his knees also.

They knelt; heads bowed, before me, as if in expectation of something, yet what that something might be was quite beyond my comprehension. Common-sense alone dictated, however, that it might be considered unwise to seriously disappoint a dozen very masculine and very naked men who had all the appearance of being warriors.

Relying on intuition alone I stepped forward the pace that the young leader had stepped back, suddenly realising that his stature, kneeling, now placed his handsome face within scarce an inch of my naked, blonde curled muff. Not knowing what else I might do I placed my hands either side of his face, stooped and kissed him on the crown of his head.

I heard him gasp and softly moan, felt him shudder, and sensed that I had somehow deeply moved him, and as thus I stood for a moment, pondering my next move somewhat hurriedly, I felt his hands alight on my buttocks, slide down and press between the rear of my thighs. Still uncertain, I fought the urge to resist and allowed my feet to slide a little apart in the sand, then struggled not to make a sound as the warrior's cock-hard, warm, soft tongue drove straight to the pink pearl focus of my gender and began to caress it moistly.

Shivering and moistening within myself I heard a collective, sussurating "Ahhh..!" then saw and realised that the others were watching quietly from their lowered eyes and, I sensed, with great approval.

Suddenly the tonguing stopped — to my relief in part, since I was beginning to find it hard to remain standing — and the young warrior stood, his face smiling warmly into mine. His hand resting softly upon my arm, he guided me gently from the spot and I scarcely drew my own gaze from those wonderful dark eyes till I found that he had placed me in front of one of his men at the furthest end of the line.

Their expectation was quite palpable and again I dropped my hands to the younger man's face, stooped down and kissed his hair. When his hands touched my arse they were shivering, almost as if in terror, and I realised what was expected. He did not find my lovely little nubble quite as quickly or adroitly as his chieftain, but for so long as his young tongue lapped questingly at my cunny I frankly cared not at all.

It is ordinarily hard to describe one's feelings and emotions in such a situation, one's knees trembling and back arching with re-action and in the quest to stay upright, the smaller hairs around and beneath one's mound tingling with a kiss of lightning, moist heat surging upwards from one's loins, flushing one's breasts and hardening the teats as all beneath the waist feels to be melt-ing into that questing mouth. Yet aside from this I had already surmised — and the renewed touch of the young chieftain's hand upon my arm confirmed it — that the second, subordinate youth was not to be the last and that, indeed, and as it proved, I was about to be tongued by every man present.

Each of them pursued his role assiduously, as soon as they had been kissed in the same manner as the others, and I must needs to clench my teeth at times that I might not cry out — sens-ing somehow they would disapprove. And it was this realisation,

I suppose, which most brought about my subsequent and correct surmise. To cry out, as I so very much desired to do, to grasp my tongues-man about the head and thrust his face up hard against my vulva, wrestle him to the ground and mount him, would prove me merely mortal and this, I had divined, was not at all what they thought me.

It was not impossible, I thought, especially given their own feral nakedness, that the act of cunnilingus might here be a normal greeting routinely offered to strange women, yet the manner of their kneeling, their hushed deportment and, most of all, the very nature of their tonguing, demonstrated something else. The caress of every tongue, whether hesitantly respectful and restrained or joyous and eager, was peculiarly gentle, delightfully submissive of themselves and felt—truly felt—the act of worship that it was.

'On account of the pallor of our skins and our general strangeness to them,' my Lord had certainly written; 'the fuzzies, on first meeting, frequently respond to us as gods, and it takes but the least endeavour, especially with the guns that they have not, to imbue them with a most proper respect for all things British.'

I had hated his pomposity, but at least—it seemed—his words were not totally inaccurate.

Quilled-cock was fourth in the order they'd assumed, close to the centre of the line, and I was surprised when, very gently, my masterful guide sought to steer me past him. I guessed that his recalcitrance ere bowing before me had caused offence to their leader, or perhaps they feared that he had caused offence to me. I, however, resisted gently, smiling, determined to make my smile forgiving, and turned to face him so closely that the hairs of my golden muff—and the scent, no doubt, of my arousal—would tickle the end of his nose.

Why, one wonders, did I do this? At worst, I suppose, I thought that I might subjugate him, compel in him the rather delightful submission to me that I had felt within the others. I already sensed that were I somehow to present it as an authoritative demand the others would have forced him into that submission whether he favoured it or not. But I wanted not to impose myself upon him thus, not least because that seamed and angry-looking visage possessed a complete set of finely chiselled and very white teeth with which, had he thought to, he could too easily and painfully have demonstrated my mortality. Instead I bowed and kissed him as the rest, very gently, perhaps lingering but a little longer. Alone and a stranger in their land I did not want to turn the hand or heart of any man against me, and since he seemed anyway thus inclined I chose not to offer him greater incitement.

His gnarled, strong hands took my buttocks in a grip that I knew would leave rosy fingertip impressions upon my skin and I felt a fluttering within my groin of panic, but when his tongue caressed me...

Perhaps it was that he sought to make me react, reveal myself as the woman I was, or perhaps it stemmed from need or desperation of his own. Whatever the cause he set my little pearl so screaming with want and hunger that I could not tell if the moisture trickling between my thighs was his or mine or both.

Only a moment or two longer and who knows what might have happened, but the chieftain steered me from Quilled-cock, and presented me to the less gifted, but still enjoyable, tongue of another of his warriors.

By the last I could barely stand, felt certain I must shortly swoon quite away in the heat and passion of my serial arousal, and I was sore afraid of what might next be demanded of me. I was not afraid that they would take me—indeed I would have been glad if they had done so and would have rejoiced to take a slim brown pizzle into every orifice I had at once, so full was I of need and longing. I was afraid, though, that they would require me to do something else, even so much as to walk with them a distance, for in the reaction of my body I was sorely weakened, could barely remain awake.

I need not, it transpired, have worried. The warriors, feeling themselves blessed and for the most part wreathed in lovely gentle smiles, now rose quietly from their knees and encircled me.

Brown hands alighted on my naked body and lifted me, others passing beneath me and joining, created a chair of muscular arms to support me, and they bore me away in reverential silence. Nor can I convey in words that lovely frisson delivered by the forearm hairs of strangers when one's naked thighs and buttocks rest, gently sliding, upon their undulating muscles, bones and sinew.

In this chair of arms they bore me, indeed, to their small and busily bustling village, where we were immediately surrounded by a curious and vivaciously chattering throng. What joy or terror, I wondered, might befall me here? Upon arrival at the village I was moved almost to tears, for I saw at first hand the paradise on which the late and unlamented Alfred had reflected. Among perhaps two hundred people with nary a stitch between them, I saw toothless old women, lean and wizened, flattened pendulous breasts pointing defeated to the floor, and one or two overly ample ones with beaming faces, their smiles mirrored in the curving creases of their darkly bolstered flesh. Old men, of course, too, whose pendant wands resembled over-thin sausages too-long cooked, and girls and boys of every age, from babes in arms to fullest flush of sturdy youth, and everywhere the firm round brown buttocks, smooth pudenda and ripe-fruit bubbies that Smythe had remembered so lasciviously.

And all of these, save those too young to know, now pressed around us, laughing and chattering among themselves, brilliant and happy as the flash of a multi-coloured parrot's wings. The sight of so many young men among them too caused me a pang of consternation, lest they were to require the same blessing as their fellows, and for a moment it looked as if they might.

All had fallen silent, gazing upon me, and at a quiet word from the chieftain those who supported my lower thighs, my legs and feet, moved a little sideways from each other to part me, opening my glistening pink maidenhood to the crowd's enraptured gaze. I could not but feel myself stirring there and pouting, and the hollowness of half-dread, half-excitement which had but recently begun to fade now began to bloom afresh and eager in my belly.

The chieftain then addressed the crowd, glancing but once or twice at me, his voice firm with authority. When he had finished I felt my buttocks clench upon the linked forearms of two of my supports as the first, a young man, approached me. At least, I thought, I am in no danger now of falling, for I remained supported by the warrior band and, indeed, I needed make not the least exertion for they simply lifted my arse, raising my quim and flooding lips towards his mouth.

This boy but nuzzled my garden a moment, then kissed me, a fleeting moist instant only, and there his blessing—it seems—was ended and he simply stepped back, smiling. This, I thought, I could cope with, yet the fact remains that after being cunny-kissed however briefly by a good three score of naked, well-proportioned and mostly handsome men, the desire and need inside myself had welled to a silent scream.

That the men were done at last offered me needed respite, till I realised that their womenfolk behind had formed a queue. Surely not! But yes, it seemed they required their blessing too—and what exquisite torture they delivered! Never had I known a woman there, and now I knew a hundred, and brief as was their homage to me it is a fact that none but a woman could express such gentleness and giving warmth so swiftly in the delicate offering of lip and tongue. I must grit my teeth, strain to keep open the eyes that demanded closure in weariness and ecstasy combined, and pray it would end swiftly.

How crude the famous measures of the ancient Inquisition, their hot irons, pliers and stretching racks, suddenly seemed, and how fortunate, perhaps, for confidentiality, that it had not occurred to such men to use a torture such as this. Not a secret in the world would I have failed to divulge had my hosts interrogated me under such poignant duress as I was now subjected to. But that was not their purpose.

Having blessed, or having been blessed by, the men and women of the settlement I was for a moment made anxious by the sight of women lifting up their children, but that it seems was for them some kind of sharing of their blessedness or an impulse to give the child a better view of me. And, all done, the moist inner shudders within my private, now very public, parts began slowly to abate and I was able to observe the better my strange and exotic surroundings.

The cluster of homes was very neat and tidy, and organised in a very orderly square around the central green where apparently untiring arms still supported me. In the middle of the green sat two great wooden, throne-like chairs, immediately adjacent a large, grey flat-topped rock which caused me sore foreboding when I observed that the grass around it was stained rather red and its surface scarred white with cleaving. A butcher's block, perhaps, I thought, yet chillingly unable to escape the presentiment that it might be both a sacrificial altar and my untimely destination.

Even as the parts of me that had been so warm became suddenly icy cold at that prospect some of the men emerged from one of the larger houses carrying between them another great, heavy chair quite similar to the other two and placed it carefully by them. To this wooden throne they now carried me, depositing me in it with infinite gentleness.

To the chair nearest mine now stepped the young chieftain and took his seat, whilst from out of the crowd came a young and deliciously pretty maid sporting a plume of soft red feathers in her head-hair. She bowed to the ground before me, then did the same to him, before stepping up to the smaller throne adjacent his.

The thrones forming a gentle curve in placement I was able to view her closely as she sat just beyond the young chief. I conjectured, correctly as it transpires, that this was his good lady and, if so, he must be counted a fortunate man. She was most petite and pretty, her brown skin and raven hair a perfect setting for the scarlet plume, and her bubbies were quite delightful on the eye, being about the scale of two good apples, no less firm, and pertly peaked. It was the garment of her nether regions, though, which I had particularly noticed, and which she wore in common with a number of others of her age and older. Though the colours differed it was but two lengths of twine, hers scarlet, one worn low around the waist and dipping below the curve of abdomen, the second tied to it before and behind and passing betwixt her legs, lying close within the cleavage of her cunny and her arse.

Like many of the younger women her maidenly attributes were rather before than beneath, an aspect perhaps exaggerated by the fact that none of them sported maiden hair in the style and quantity to which one is accustomed, their mounds being decorated by a slender, close rivulet of hair most unlike our own. Much of the forward part of her lower lips, therefore, was clearly to be seen, and the narrow scarlet thong passed quite obviously between them. One could not but wonder at the purpose of such a slender, poignant garment, and it was only very much later that I learned its proper meaning, that it defined consent. A consenting woman, I would learn in time, removes the thong altogether. Displacing the thong, to one or another side in order to affect entry, they consider by definition rape.

Late in a day which had begun with myself anticipating brutal rape, had included my sending an unfortunate man to a somewhat ghastly end and which, not yet concluded, had bestowed upon me a surfeit of quite delicious but as yet unrequited cunnilingus, it is hardly to be thought strange that I found myself sinking into reverie, wondering in part whether all this was a dream I might wake from in my malodorous shipboard cabin. It was not. Raised voices stirred me.

Quilled-cock was stalking up and down before his chieftain in obvious distress, with lowering brows and pouting lips, repeatedly gesticulating toward one of the larger houses. Gazing in the direction in which he pointed I saw to my surprise quite a caravan of men and women, some engaged in carrying into the house all the contents from my boat and not a few engaged in carrying other objects out.

It dawned upon me suddenly that they were displacing this old fellow on my behalf, moving me into, and expelling him from, what was obviously his home. This, for some reason, I felt I could not abide, and rising slowly, wearily, from my seat, I walked somewhat unsteadily toward the scene of activity. Intervening in the queue of carriers I first folded my arms and shook my head, then pointed to the rather pathetic pile of goods on the ground and gestured that they attend to it, pointing into the house to make my purpose known.

I could feel the curiosity of two hundred pairs of eyes fixed upon my naked form, could hear the silence. Then the chieftain spoke, his tone very firm, and hands equally firm took hold of my shoulders and drew me out of the way. The porterage recommenced immediately, my goods moving inexorably into the house, the old man's equally inexorably out of it.

Shrugging-off the warm hands that rested firm and yet unthreatening on my shoulders, and not entirely unconscious of the accidental caress upon my buttocks of my restrainer's member, I stood and watched for a moment or two then turned and moved to the small discard pile that represented poor Quilled-cock's belongings. There being too much for me to lift alone and at once I turned to the warrior who had restrained me and pointed, then stooped and lifted what I could—principally a bundle of furs. This I, unrestrained, then carried into the house, depositing it to one side of the large and largely empty room within.

My goods—poor Alfred's goods as were—were stacked neatly in the corner and, so far as I could tell, were completely untampered-with. Close by, on the floor, lay a large pile of dry grass draped with two coverlets of fur very similar to that which I'd just brought in. My very being guessed its purpose and, weary past belief and caring, without so much as a fleeting thought for the symbolism inherent in my having just carried a strange man's bed into what was now, apparently, my home, I lay myself down and drifted swiftly off to sleep.

Chapter the Third

In which June and Summer acquire an even warmer aspect.

I awoke naked, slick and sweating from a dark dream of a
ship becalmed, still and stifling, dream-reek of perspiring
sailors, rum and tar in my nostrils, to a dream of stillness,
a distant gentle bustle, cool morning light. And this was not a
dream, my walls still of woven slender bamboo-like poles, my
ceiling still the peaceful green of thatch-work fronds.

The other bed had gone, and remembrance of the old man's
unwonted eviction fleetingly annoyed me, brought a frown to
my face. And only then did it strike me that my act in bringing in
what was patently his bed might—however inadvertently—have
suggested to my new hosts an immoral purpose. It occurred to
me suddenly that I might have given very grave offence to people
who, thus far, had done nothing whatever to harm me—however
strange and poignant their benisons toward me. Sitting up slowly and looking about me I saw two further beds in a corner of the
room and two young girls, of late teen-age perhaps, sitting upon
them watching me, clearly curious. Then a fleeting movement at
the open doorway of someone standing hidden from me by the
wall, disclosed to me first one and then another armed warrior,
clearly set to guard me.

Had my faux pas with the bed made them my enemies? Was
I now a prisoner here? Or was that anyway my destiny? Was
the rest merely some taunting precursor to ritual disembowel-
ment—or some similar delight—upon that terrible stone? Lost in
alien strangeness, I was fleetingly much afraid.

Seeing me awake, though, the girls now sprang to life, animated grins upon their faces, animated chatter causing at least
one of the doorway guards to turn his head. The first of the girls,
whose name I would later learn was something like Sum-Mah
and who was pleased for me to call her 'Summer' ever thereafter, hurried towards me with a wooden platter and presented me

with breakfast. I barely know what it was I ate and into which I dipped my cautious fingers, no eating utensils being in evidence, save that part of it was most succulent fish, but I know I've never eaten better. The second girl, whom again I later came to know as 'Joo-Oon' and was forever 'June' to me, brought a flask and cup carved of coconut husk and served me an unknown drink composed of coconut milk and more.

Their happy, laughing faces no less restorative to me than the food and drink they had supplied, suggested to me that I was in no immediate danger, whilst their subsequent games quite rendered me a child again. Without a word and scarce a deed in common, yet desperate to communicate, we had no other choice at first save to rely on pantomime. Humour-full as this proved to be, the need quickly decided me to learn all of their language that I could (though had I been a man, of course, I would have insisted that they all learn mine!) and I began in earnest straight away.

Animated and joyous as the two girls were, there was in their demeanour towards me a very marked respect and I remained quite sure that they thought me still a goddess or spirit of some sort. Was it odd, I wondered, that they brought a goddess food and drink? But then, of course, I realised it was not, knowing even from my learning—far more scant than it should be—that many cultures place gifts of food and drink at shrines. This provoked a deeper question: just how human might they expect their goddess to be? For I knew a time must come when I must engage in the most vulnerable of human acts and I wondered how they would perceive those.

Odd, is it not, that I can write of fucking and of cunnilingus with scarce a thought of propriety or embarrassment, yet those other actions seem to deny easy transition into words. 'Making water', I suppose, is discreet enough for one, but how on earth does one describe the other function in good taste?

I need not, in fact, have worried, discovering my hosts to be the earthiest of people who said prayers to the god of a fruit-delivering tree and thought nothing then of pissing against it or planting their motions beneath it. But the matter was not, shall we say, discreet.

It surprises me still that they were so quick to determine my woeful ignorance and that, believing me a goddess or spirit of some kind they seemed entirely unsurprised by it. Arising from my bed I walked around the hut—or rather, house, for hut suggests something a great deal more crude—picking up and touching a number of items, gesturing to the whole and bringing to my face a look of such complete perplexity and curiosity as I could devise.

Sensing my need with an alacrity that would always subsequently surprise me, Summer and June took it upon themselves to show me everything they could—our long bamboo table upon its trestles which had the function of a sideboard only, for we ate upon the floor, implements for eating and drinking, a water gourd and carved wooden bowl for washing, necessaries of all such kind.

There remained but one small group of items clustered in a corner of the floor and having managed to make it clear that I had understood all else through their demonstrations and pantomimes, I pointed toward these items and raised a questioning eyebrow. They comprised a large wooden bowl with a number of other, smaller, bowls and a gourd beside it, a short, broad leaf the size of serving platter and a pile of sponges near. I remember watching the girls standing, gazing down upon it with perplexity evident in both their faces. Pantomime was the outcome.

Slender Summer took what was to be my part, pointing first to me and then to herself and then secreting behind the largest bowl a small cup of water from the washing gourd. Placing a foot each side of the bowl she lowered herself to a squatting position, clearly struggling to ignore June's giggles, and after a moment palmed the water cup and trickled its contents between her legs till it plashed in the basin beneath her. She then looked up at me and I nodded comprehension and waited as she set aside the cup, before requiring me to try to watch without collapsing into laughter as she pantomimed a face of epic straining, as if in the throes of most terrible constipation.

After a moment or two of this, during which chubby little June could be seen rolling naked around the floor quite beside herself with merriment, Summer lifted her lovely little buttocks, peered myopically down into the bowl and gave a smile of inordinate satisfaction as one who had delivered herself of a tremendous burden. As Summer rose to her feet, June stepped forward, covered the bowl and its imaginary contents with the large leaf and, stooping, dipped a sponge into the prepared smaller bowl of water alongside.

Kneeling down close to her partner June then proceeded to wipe the other girl from stem, as it were, to stern, dallying at the 'stem' perhaps a little longer than she might, and on finishing at the stern she deposited the 'soiled' sponge in another smaller, empty basin . Their pantomime over, both girls now grinned at me, waiting for my reassurance that I'd understood, which I gave them by smiling and nodding. Yet much as I nodded and smiled still they shook their heads, and it was only after considerable gesturing that I began to understand. They wanted me to enact my own part.

To have been in real need might have made it easier and yet, for some reason, I was not, but to act the part out before them took all of my self possession. I had, after all, always been taught that this was the most private matter for ladies, denied the freedom to piss in that pot which post-prandial gentlemen shared and kept in the dining-room sideboard, and there could nowhere in the world exist a less private situation than that in which I found myself. The brittle apprehension of what they sought of me, the knowledge that I must appear—most to myself—ridiculous, the belly-knotting anticipation of inexorably threatening embarrassment, promised even now to turn my legs to jelly.

For one thing the guards at the doorway could hear every word and sound which occurred in the room and were not above glancing within, and the doorway too was a doorway and open, uncovered, providing an unhindered view to anyone passing. The girls' nakedness and my own I had scarcely begun to adjust to, still being startled from time to time by accidents of their posture which no swift aversion of my gaze could prevent from disclosing, however briefly, the glorious pinkness of pouting vulva or sweet, clean roundness of little brown sphincter.

I could not resist their blandishments, however, and found myself poised in a most inelegant pantomime crouch above the freshly uncovered pot. I had not thought to avail myself of a cup of water as Summer had, but that little devil was not to be cheated and as June drew my glance with an unexplained giggle Summer herself quite drenched my maidenhood with a sudden douche of water. In the ambient warmth the douche seemed keenly cold as it swirled over and under my mound ere cascading into the bowl. Both irritated and—despite myself—amused, I made my simulated motion so swiftly that they shook their heads in pretended disbelief, and I was not to be spared the cleansing.

They shook their heads as I reached for the sponge bowl, their countenances suddenly serious, and I as swiftly realised the import of it. This was their role, not mine, and I could not deter them from it without causing grave offence. So I submitted, then and thereafter when the action involved no pretence, and I have to record the subtle joy of that sensation, of two gently applied sponges teasing and cleansing the twin orifices of one's joy and waste.

The game concluded to their satisfaction, the two girls led me outside and round the corner of the house, enabling me to observe that the two guards remained where they were and made no move to follow. Behind the house, beyond two ordered rows of village homes and across a small meadow, I was led to the shallows of a gentle stream where other villagers were bathing, male and female together. Children played and splashed in the shallows, two warriors watching over all and observant of any danger, and the shrub enshrouded shallows echoed with the laughter of children, the happy voices of our people, and the song of birds and insects. Eden could have known no greater joy or beauty.

The other villagers bathed themselves, of course, but June

and Summer insisted on bathing me, treating me again to that lovely intimacy of caressing hands and lying together with me afterwards in the grass as we waited for the sun to dry us.

Returning to the house, the first of our callers was waiting, no less a man than the chief himself, his badge of office and only dress a tall black and white feather. And if he had been waiting long he gave no sign of it, bestowing on me only his wonderful, melting smile.

Of all the men I had thus far seen, and of those I could recollect, given the piquantly arduous and exhausting circumstances of the previous day, there was none whose appearance, demeanour and character had made quite so great an impact on me. Only among bare-knuckle prize fighters whose bouts occurred occasionally at fairs nearby to my childhood home had I ever witnessed such a physique, the square, hard-looking chest, the undulating curves of muscle rippling below it to the smooth flatness of belly and groin, the vein ribbed curvature of arm and muscular thigh. And even in repose, when in fact none of the village men that I ever saw displayed quite the shrivelled state of repose which I had seen on English men, his member remained of quite mouth-watering dimensions.

And no prize-fighter that I ever saw ever had so handsome and finely chiselled a face, nor such large eyes, nor seemed to contain within himself such a remarkable inner strength, purpose and confidence. I had noted already, among the many impressions of the previous evening, that he seemed scarcely able to glance at man, woman or child without a wondrous gentle smile playing about his lips, like a father blessed by his children. My having scarcely met him or begun to know him my own inner voices were able to declare that this was a most loving man, and I had always thereafter to fight an impulse to throw myself into those strong protective arms, to kiss him upon those warm, firm lips.

Finding him now in my home and quite ignorant of what he might want of me, I waited for an explaining mime or gesture and suddenly noticed that his wife was present. She too smiled, though it seemed to me a little nervously.

Arshon, as I came to know him, coughed—quite unnecessarily—to gain my attention and then placed in my hands two objects. Both of these were figurines, one long and slender and freshly carved—it seemed to me—from white wood. I knew immediately that the body represented was mine, for though the bust was proportionately larger than my own, the hips proportionately wider, there was no mistaking the facial features or the delicately carved weight of flowing curls. The second figure was worn with age, cut from darker wood and clearly represented an infant. I do not think I've ever seen a sweeter object, nor felt such warmth emanate from one.

Had the chief come, then, to bring me gifts? I thought not, from his diffident and somewhat uncomfortable manner and posture. Summer and June were my guides again, June taking me by the hand and gently drawing me towards my bed, which had been re-laid in the centre of the room. Arshon's wife approached me now, entirely naked and carrying her thong in her hand. A taut little smile on her lips she then lay down upon her back on my bed.

Summer, at hand, smiled gently at me and no-less gently reached down and under and touched me lightly twixt my legs, her gaze scarcely parting from my questioning eyes. And having touched me she moved the same hand slowly till it caressed the lips of the girl on the bed. A blessing, then, but different in posture?

Not sure how to begin I felt June and Summer's hands upon my upper arms, gently coaxing me downward. Finding no other way I knelt, placing my knees either side of the recumbent girl's head, lowering my vulva toward her face, arching back with the suddenness of her moist contact, her tongue upon my clitoris.

Seeing me almost fallen the two girls knelt beside me, cradling me between them, and the warrior's princess between my legs continued her gentle lapping. Only then did I see that Arshon too was lowering himself to the ground. With no clothing to divest himself of, but his feather gone, and wearing but a different pattern—I seemed to think—of paint, I could plainly see his statuesque and enviable erection, watch in warm fascination as he slid it effortlessly into her, his wife.

And as he did her mouth closed on me, sighing, for I felt the rush of air around and within my parts, and all of me was now consumed by her, enveloped in her moistness. Between my thighs her head rocked slowly back and forth to the pattern of his gentle thrusting and between her lips her sweet tongue probed, now, thrusting wetly into me with a rhythm that matched his own.

What words have I to describe that feeling? The strangeness of having a woman there, not imparting as the others had the night before some fleeting kiss, but nuzzling and licking, tonguing and suckling, whilst I watched her husband's very cock slide back and forth within her lovely slit, heard the wet sounds of their congress even as I heard and felt those on my cunny? Such a heat there came within me, such a fire of wanting in this strangeness, and yet I knew I must suppress it, that I could not appear to them the human that I was.

Supporting himself on his iron-sinewed arms, the living and beautiful mahogany carving that was Arshon's face hung often close to mine, eyes closed, muscles tense with concentration, till at the last his face reached out to mine, his lips found my lips and he kissed me, deeply, long and sweetly, his tongue probing me, her tongue probing me, and both to the rhythm of his lovely pounding cock.

'Twas her he was kissing, of course, and I was but their medium. I felt him coming even as she did, felt the gushing of him in the clenching moistness of the mouth that held me in her, in the arching of her body and the thudding of her face into my groin, and in a sudden inner gushing of my own.

As soon as he was come the girls drew me upward and away, and I watched as he subsided onto her, took her in his arms. I envied her so, and June and Summer, I know, saw it. Sweet Summer raised a hand before my face and showed me the carving of myself. As near as she could within the scale of it she kissed the figure on the groin, then opened her other hand to show the second, baby, figure. And somehow I understood. Arshon and his wife desired a baby, presumably had done so for a while, and offerings to other gods having been to no avail they had availed themselves of me. I was fertility.

Flattering as that seemed in its way to me, it left me with a problem.

In that other life, which had within days come to seem an impossibly distant memory, I had been loved, fucked and charmingly taken on a number of occasions, and though most of it was fun, most of it too was tinged with disappointment. This had much to do with Sam, the beautifully muscled stable-lad who had lent his glory to my youth.

With many men I'd known heat and passion, and many had brought me to that liquid brink which seemed almost to peak with a sudden molten gushing inside and out of me, and yet not quite. I always felt that there was a point beyond which I never reached, and indeed I knew that it was so, for I had reached that truly wondrous point almost every time with Sam.

My second lover, after the one-time loveless business with Squire Smailes which took my maidenhood, Sam was the only man I could not know enough of. Having watched him from afar, as it were, for a matter of several weeks, I encountered him one hot and very sunny day whilst he was brushing down the mare that father gave me.

Sam was stripped down to the waist, on account of the summer heat, wearing only knee-breeches and shoes so that his legs were anyway mostly bare, and his breeches reposed very low on his hips on account of his so-slender waist. Not seeing me immediately I had the opportunity to watch his movement, watch the rippling, sweat-glossy, golden muscles of his arms, back and shoulders, and notice—on account of his low slung breeches— the beginning cleft and pale extremities of his lovely girl-round arse.

I knew immediately that I wanted him and, catching the expression on his face as he looked up, knew well that he was unlikely to cause obstruction. As he straightened to look at me—and he looked so very and unabashedly directly, not at all as a servant should look—I noticed the breadth of his chest, the light mat of hair that on him looked charming rather than gross, the rippling curves of muscle of his abdomen.

"A fine beast," he commented, patting the horse's haunch.

"I was thinking the very same," I answered lightly, keeping my gaze upon him.

"Your father is a fine judge of horseflesh."

"'Twas not the horse of which I spoke."

He smiled, knowing:

"I guessed 'twere not."

"Besides," quoth I; "she is a mare, and fine enough, but I am in the market for a champion stallion, a racer and stud, hard, fast and able to stay the course!"

"Takes a good judge of horseflesh to choose a good stallion," he answered, clearly teasing.

"I think I know enough to be an adequate judge of flesh, be it horse or other." I answered him, quite delighted with the direction and tenor of this verbal exchange, with the sparkle of laughter and want in his eyes.

He straightened up, puffed out his chest a little, grinning:

"And would my lady buy this stallion?"

"Not without closer inspection. Blanketed as he is I could not well enough judge how pleasing he would be to the mare I have in mind."

We were both emboldened, I must advise, by a general dearth of company. My father and my brother were elsewhere, many servants away at a fair and those who were not were quite busy enough in other parts of the house and grounds, unlikely to find us.

"My lady wishes to judge the beast?" he asked me slyly.

"Afore I'll make my choice, yes," I answered lightly, seeking to tease him with my grand, practised, most nonchalant smile.

Grinning boldly he began to shuck his breeches down and I followed their slow movement with my eyes, watching the dark rivulet of hair that trickled from his navel grow into a lovely triangle of promise.

And what appeared at the triangle's base was, in its arousal, frankly magical, a good man's hand-length, and wide around, endearingly eager, flushed and bald where it thrust from his foreskin.

"A bargain," I said; "I'll take it." And I did too, and often.

Squire Smailes having had that manly propensity to fuck for his own enjoyment alone, being rogered by Sam was a joyous education. When the Squire had bade me suck his wick I had declined, disliking its stubby, pale proportions, but when Sam asked—and he did ask so gently—I found myself unconscionably eager. I loved its weight, loved the twin hard walnuts of its sacs, the way it stretched my lips and inner mouth, frankly adored its cascading taste. And to have that joy inside me—the very memory makes me wet.

A yard by common name, it felt a veritable yard within me, pushing and thrusting, delightfully stretching, somehow stroking something within me that which no other prong or hand or instrument ever afterwards reached, filling my loins with a sensation of lightning, flickering brightly, fluttering softly, fountaining its inundation as I fountained my own and warming me at once from cunny to teat, finally exploding in my head so fiercely that I screamed in fear of imminent death.

Lovely little death, how I did miss thee! How I did miss the trickling wetness in thigh joints and arse-cleft, chilling softly as the shocked, warm mind returns to function.

It could not last. A matter of station, of course, and of change, of debutantisme and coming-out, of public show, of dowry and of marriage prospect.

Sam would marry Ginny, and she, the seed merchant's daughter, would garner all of my Samuel's seed and make, by all accounts, a number of fat, healthy babies from it. I, but days after their wedding, departed for London, Society and a surfeit of disappointment.

A number of men would congratulate themselves upon the

efficacy of their penile endeavours as a result of that flooding of mine which they took as testament of their success. But this it was not, merely a trick of nature played cruelly upon me and leaving me so often wanting.

Minnarra, my chieftain's princess, even now appeared as one having just emerged from a heavy rain, the front of her hair and her face full wet from tears, from sweat, from mouth-fluids of her own that had run from my groin and from that self-same inundation of mine, no doubt, and he was kissing all, and tasting all, in such an effulgence of love. But I had not screamed, had not near-died. I had not come.

And drawn so close, again, as I had been but yesterday time after time after time, the need had become a weight like cannon-shot within my loins and it felt as if every single point upon my skin which could be touched and feel lay upon the brink of some kind of seizure, silently, madly screaming for release.

All this, somehow, the two girls knew, and as Arshon and his glad wife departed, taking the carven doll-baby with them, such a look passed across Summer's face that I wondered at its fury.

Yet it was gone when she turned to me, came to me and embraced me.

Of all the manifest novelties of this new life, so many and so soon, I remember this so vividly. I had never been held by a woman before, save with the walls of clothing, manners and propriety between us, and being held by her and June as I was then was something most astonishing.

As tall as myself, yet ever so slender, Summer placed her arms around me, tilted her head and laid it on my shoulder. If that embrace itself were strange, the pressure of her small firm bubbies and their tiny teats against the soft flesh of my own, the sweet press of belly on belly, the gentle kissing friction of her mound on mine, were quite extraordinary. And when the smaller June embraced us both, laying her soft face against my other shoulder, the firmness of her teats pressing gently into me, the curve of her belly moulding to the curve of my lower back and her mound so soft in the cleavage of my bottom, I shook with the so-sweet

warmth of it and found myself weeping, turning my head even
as I wept to kiss their recumbent cheeks. And they wept, too, I
knew not why, and kissed my shoulders, my neck, my cheeks,
bestowing the wetness of their tears, and none of this as lovers
lusting, only as lovers gentling, aiding.

I know, now, that they ached as I did, when time and need
bade us draw apart, ended that embrace, and yet in moments
they were playful again, laughing and bright and joyous, killing
the darkness that lay inside me with the light of their glorious,
incandescent spirits.

Knowing it does not do to dwell and that being busy can put
all else to flight, I determined now, in the absence of callers, to
turn my hand to a matter which had greatly occupied my mind
and I turned my attention to my stock of goods.

The whiskey I ignored, having little predilection for the stuff,
but noting that one of the kegs was differently marked I opened
its spigot and discovered a good brandy which I soon put to restorative use. Other things I already knew of I likewise set aside,
but I was determined to examine a particular trunk of inordinate
size and weight. I was glad to have done so, for I found all manner of astonishing things within. One was a bible for which, I
must be frank, I have always had little use, another a cased pair
of very fine and monogrammed pistols to add to that which I
had removed from Alfred's breeches, together with powder
horn, flints, a kit for cleaning and for making shot. There was,
too, a small package of blank lead to use with the latter, a modest
amount that would not go far, but I had seen little requirement
for firearms thus far here in paradise.

That Smythe's trunk was not his own but was a package with
a quite select destination with which he had been charged delivery, was immediately suggested by the monogrammed guns
whose case had lain almost at the top, but the items beneath
it swiftly confirmed that conclusion. There were several men's
shirts and a richly brocaded waistcoat, all bearing the mark of
an esteemed London tailor, together with two pair of elegantly
tailored breeches. Beneath these, to my pleasure, were several

very fine petticoats of lawn, all of them rolled tight to form a soft packing around a fine looking box, mahogany inlaid with fine metals and ivory.

The contents of this box were, I may say, of great joy to me, since the main part and the many tiny, delicately decorated drawers contained within it, disclosed only the most wonderful items of a lady's toilette—perfumes and cologne in crystal bottles, powders and colours in charming little inlaid boxes, and a wonderful set of brushes, mirror and combs.

And below that box was another treasure yet, of three fine dresses clearly destined for a lady. For a little while at least I was in Heaven, able to see and repair myself as a lady should and with a prospect, anyway, of at some time dressing in the manner to which I had long been accustomed.

I will not list the contents entire of the treasure trove the late Alfred unwillingly bequeathed me, only mention that it contained many other things of use and potential, the latter including two smaller casks of which one was powder, one shot.

In respect of all these things my two delightful girls showed every expression of joy, though it was clear to me that their joy arose entirely from my own and had nothing to do with the quality and quantity of my new possessions, many of which were mysteries to them. A tinder-box did amaze them, truly, but it was the bales of cloth and packets of beads which moved them most, and I made sure to establish the particular favourites of each as soon as I could and bestow them as gifts.

One piece of saffron fabric seemed to have them both in thrall, and since it was by far the largest—being wrapped around the contents of one bale—I was quite prepared to pare it into two. This they both resisted vehemently, which I found strange, only then after some animated and smiling discussion between them I was astonished to witness their taking the fabric and fastening it—after a brief conversation with the guards—to the upper frame off the doorway. Admitting its own saffron-tinted light and a subtle play of external shadows this simple curtain, simply placed, gave me that which I had most been lacking. I had my privacy. And its efficacy in this regard was very soon proved for—perhaps in consequence of that brief conversation—the guards, who had been in the free habit of glancing into the room, now took to rapping their spear-shafts against the doorpost as a signal of intention and waiting for one of the girls to respond.

The curtain in place I was tempted to try-on one of the gowns for my own interest and the girls' possible amusement, but I found I could not bring myself to do so. Given our new, limited privacy, I discovered with some amazement, I became poignantly aware of yet greater joy in my freedom, and June, Summer and I limited our experiments with clothing to wrapping pieces of coloured material about our bodies and dancing.

The bodies I had embraced and which had embraced mine were not in any sense child-like, and already in little looks and gestures I had seen and sensed a maturity and intelligence in both of these young women at least the equal of my own. Yet dancing in floating veils of coloured muslin they were so much—in their lightness and joy—as children, and I, in their company, so much a happy child again.

But that could not last forever. A rap on the doorpost announcing a visitor we swiftly, if reluctantly, returned our fabrics to their corner and settled ourselves, Summer advancing to the door as envoy and drawing the curtain aside, June drawing me towards my bed and indicating I should sit.

Waiting patiently in the doorway and smiling broadly was Gorrogo, my old friend Quilled-cock himself.

Chapter the Fourth

In which a little man's 'little man'
produces joy beyond proportion.

Given recent anxieties and my great concern and dismay at his summary eviction, I can admit to being rather relieved at discovering Gorrogo, as I would come to know his name, in a seeming happy state upon my doorstep. Responding to my own very genuine smile of welcome he now stepped into the house, pausing to nod at the golden drape and deliver a grin of evident approval. Aside from mine, I would learn in time, only two doorways in the village bore a covering of any kind. One was the chieftain's, the other Gorrogo's, both door-coverings comprising sewn-together skins of small and valued animals, and both indicative of their status—Arshon's as King, Gorrogo's as Priest, or Medicine Man.

I had correctly surmised the nature of Gorrogo's employment long before it was confirmed to me, based upon his manner, conduct and—if one can call it such—his 'dress', and had guessed that till my arrival he had been their most special intermediary between themselves and their gods. I felt him likely to have seen me, therefore, as a most unwelcome usurper, and a dire threat to his position, from the very beginning.

At an indication from Summer, Gorrogo now sat down before me and placed upon the expanse of bed between us a package wrapped in small furs of brilliant gold and black and white. Still smiling warmly, and appearing very happy, he proceeded to open the package that I might view its contents and then, with arms uplifted, palms wide open, he clearly presented all to me.

I would later learn that he was entirely genuine, though now I thought him a little suspect. He was astonished and deeply gratified, it turned out, at my gestures of the previous evening, interceding in his behalf and then carrying-in his bed. It is perhaps fortunate that I did not know that that latter action had conveyed to all an offer of marriage on my part which, fortunately and for reasons politic, he had felt it necessary to decline.

On the king's intercession also, resulting much from those events, Gorrogo had been given another house close by, only slightly lower in status (since it did not sit directly opposite that of the king), and very much to his liking, and had been diplomatically reassured of his own role in the village. Deciding that I was a spiritual representation of love and fertility, a veritable Aphrodite as it were, it was only associated duties which were to be apportioned to me, whilst the medicinal, prophetic and other duties which had always been Gorrogo's would remain so.

Unwittingly, thus, I had happily relieved him of a portion of his labour, and he was of no mind to resent it. Moreover, I would discover, not only did he feel and acknowledge a genuine debt of gratitude for acts of kindness to him, but I had done him another act of kindness which I might, at some times, have regretted.

As I was to discover, representing fertility imposed by custom upon its representative a life of effectual celibacy. Like me he had, whilst representing that which I now represented, been given his own attendants, but in his case they were two strapping youths whose principal religious function was to milk him when required, sucking and masturbating him to a point at which he ejaculated into a cup. The contents of the cup—I am sure to no delight of his own—were then imbibed a sip at a time between the supplicant and himself.

No longer responsible for matters of fecundity, sexual prowess or arousal, his boys had been replaced by a single female attendant whose duty was to fulfil his every need and desire. In consequence he was a far, far happier man, and the lady concerned was to walk bow-legged for weeks.

The contents of the package, then, represented—though I fully understood it not—a double gift. First and foremost was a bundle of the most glorious and spectacular feathers I had ever set eyes upon and which set my girls to swooning, and these were simply a rather special and very generous personal offering. Beneath these, and of no less import, lay a collection of artefacts and materials which he had collected and assembled during the time of his previous responsibility and which, as his successor, he was now content to pass on to me.

These included a rather frightening looking knife, a forearm's length overall, which was unusual in having a metal blade (almost all of their tools were wood or bone) and the handle of which—forming half its length—had been intricately carved in the shape of a phallus. There were packets of small leaves and herbs, too, pouches and horn-casks of coloured powders, an extraordinary headdress of yet more feathers with a projecting, life-size, sculpted penis to the fore, a long slim pouch of the thinnest animal skin, the use of which I quickly conjectured, it being very similar in some ways to items I had known, a large flask of oil, many other things besides, and two last objects worthy of special mention:

One of these appeared at first glance to be an odd-shaped bowl containing a strange inner protrusion, but which, inverted, revealed itself to be a disconcertingly accurate yet quite charming sculpture of the female loins. Of wood inside, the outer surface was gently padded, covered over in soft animal hide impeccably modelled and moulded to form a female cunny. Complete with padded pubis and soft pouting lips, that which had appeared to protrude out of the device did in fact intrude within it, and was a sealed internal tube or channel, also made of hide.

Sensing my curiosity—and, had I but known it, enjoying his new freedom—Gorrogo picked the sculpture up, mimicked pouring a few drops of oil from the flagon and, grinning, inserted his member, already noticeably aroused, into the false vulva and the enclosing channel, before withdrawing it slowly and with every sign of pleasure. Clearly—I knew—'twas a tosser's delight.

The second object was closely related, a model penis so skilfully made that I wondered at first if it were real and had been severed from some hapless victim. On closer inspection, however, it became happily clear that it was but a carving, however exquisitely detailed, and formed of good size with a very sweet upward curve. Overall it had a form similar to a club, possessing a straight wooden handgrip where the masculine groin would have been, and a crossbar much as a knife might have had save that this was curved and padded above in a fake pubis with two heavy, false testes below. A tosser's delight again, I knew, only this time for a woman, or perhaps some man or woman who preferred sex a-la-derrière for all that I could tell.

Rather having sensed, by now, the kind of duties for which I might be called upon, this generous gift already appeared most promising to me, and I was frankly lost to know quite how to respond to it. Even the girls seemed to be at a loss, for I looked to them in vain for a solution.

The means by which I chose to thank him was not—given my ignorance—without some risk, I suppose. The only chairs in the village comprising the three graven thrones, Gorrogo and I were both seated, squatting, upon my bed on the floor. In our mutual nakedness, therefore, there was little of each other that was hidden from our view, and whilst I was conscious that much of the time he could barely take his gaze from the little pink slit that could not but gape twixt knees apart, I could also not but see the engorgement of his manhood, rising warmly upward like the bowsprit of a ship.

For all that Gorrogo was not young—the grey in his hair and the lines of his visage made that clear—I cannot say he was unhandsome, being lean and spare, wirily muscular and toned, and I felt deeply moved and gratified by the actions of this man who could so easily have been mine enemy. Thus moved I lowered myself to my knees before him, leaned easily forward and kissed him on the exposed tip that pointed so expectantly upward towards me. Just a kiss, and I hunkered back upon my heels, reached out one hand and held him.

I saw astonishment on his face, and a plenitude of genuine pleasure, and hearing no murmur or gasp of shock from the girls who stood watching, smiling gently on the periphery of my vision, I began to ply him, gently. I felt the girls subside beside us, kneeling like myself, felt Summer's hand slide beneath my buttocks, her fingers brush my lips and stay there, playing. June placed her hand, meanwhile, round the very base of the cock I was plying, pressing gently on his balls, clearly mindful of the quill's sharp tip. She did not move though, and seemed simply to be awaiting something.

Gorrogo, awkward on his haunches, had sunk onto his knees, his head and shoulders back-tilted, pure delight upon his face, and sensing the moment in the sudden joyous tension of that expression I began to ply him harder, stroking backward, forward and over the silken, now barely moistened, tip.

June suddenly moved her hand, her finger tip pushing firmly down in order to depress and guide him, her other hand appearing under mine with one of our carven cups and into this Gorrogo exploded, liquid and gushing, filling the tiny cup to the rim.

Please God, I thought—with less immediate alarm than I might have experienced had I known the medicinal properties my new friends' culture ascribed to such actions—that I am not expected to drink it! Warm and expressed in manly gushing is one thing, tepid from a cup surely something else!

Gorrogo sighed, his head sinking forward on his chest, clearly satiated, and we left him thus a moment, June reaching to put her arm about his shoulders. When he recovered, looking up and smiling gently, I was astonished to see tears in his eyes.

He quietly arose, scarce taking his gaze from my face even as June presented him with the cup. He kept it with him, in the manner I suppose of a precious souvenir, covering it with one hand as he held it in the other, and now—his expression wondering—he left us, backing slowly toward the door, not turning away till the curtain fell behind him.

Left alone, the girls and I submitted his gifts to closer inspection, and the girls in particular seemed almost beside themselves with joy. How they knew all that they knew is beyond my speculation, yet the fact is that nothing present seemed a mystery to them, and they would turn that to my advantage.

More moved than aroused, though quietly missing Summer's playful hand upon me, I was already feeling weary, yet the day seemed scarce begun and almost as soon as Gorrogo had gone there was a rapping on the doorpost. Summer, bless her, answered it, and though I knew not what was said I could not but conjecture that it was of little import, since she allowed the curtain to fall behind her as she returned and there was no further importuning for the moment.

Instead they fed me, then they washed me, bidding me lie upon the bed whilst they did so. Since I had been involved in no great exertion, nor splashed by Gorrogo's coming, I can but assume that they did it to refresh me, and that they did, caressing every inch of my body with soft, damp sponges. Did they dally longer than they needed when they refreshed those aching parts betwixt my legs? I am not sure; I only know how much I loved their soft attention.

It did occur to me to wonder then whether I had been gifted with these two girls because they were of that unmentionable kind, women who are lovers of women, against whom I had long been taught to nurture disdain and disgust—and not I, alone. What our Lords and Masters deemed unnatural acts in those days had at times brought women to the pillory to suffer the cruellest abuse at the hands of affronted Christian folk and had brought many men to the gallows. And I had never questioned those prejudices, any more than I had questioned the right of my class to bend and twist every commandment I had learned by rote from the pulpit of my church.

Now, though, I found that I burned with an inner anger, against myself, and cursed my own stupidity. I had bent and broken every moral law and restriction in finding pleasure or purpose with men, I had learned full well that the marital union so beloved of the law-makers could be a most invidious and disgusting institution, and I had, I knew, experienced no small amount of pleasure when cunny-tongued under the gentlest restraint by upwards of a hundred women, and whilst enjoying the tender toilette ministrations of these two, self-same, lovely young girls.

In that defining moment it occurred to me that I cared neither jot nor tittle any longer about the sexual predilections of my species, save for those like the Smythes, Smailes and others who know only their own gratification, abuse others in freedom of power or wilfully and despitefully cause pain to others who do not wish it and cannot prevent it. At the same time, too, I somehow realised that these two girls were not of that Greek fashion, or if they were, were not of that particular bent alone.

They had given and gave me pleasure, took pleasure in gentling me and especially those parts of me that were made for gentling, but the pleasure they took was quite clearly simply loving. Whilst it was obvious that they viewed my body and its extremities with pleasure, respect and even admiration, neither their looking nor touching at any time smacked to me of lusting, only ever, and wonderfully, of giving.

Such reflections were too soon ended, for as I lay there cooled and gazing upon their sweet brown bodies the guards rapped again at the doorpost and I knew I was recalled to duty.

Sweet Summer my door-keeper again now introduced, holding the cloth aside for their passage, a slight and somehow browbeaten—but not unhandsome—looking man and a woman who towered, in truth, both around and above him. There was indeed enough human material in her form to have made perhaps three of considerable buxomness and, in consequence of her extreme largeness being composed about a normal frame, looked rather as if she had started some three times taller and had been compressed, causing the flesh to concertina about her.

Imposing as the woman was, even as she sat rather pooling upon the floor, and timid as seemed the man, one could not but observe the loveliness in her face. Not laughing now, one could see that her face was quite made to be so and that it must have laughed long and loud to produce the lines that it had.

What, though, could be their problem, I wondered as both sat gazing at me, clearly in expectation? June came, this time, to my rescue. Placing herself behind them and out of their sight, whilst yet directly in my own, she produced both the long-handled wooden phallus that Gorrogo had brought and the sculpted bowl vagina. Raising a pointing finger toward the man she placed the phallus, handle first, within the very cleavage of her mound and, holding the artificial cunny a brief distance from her wooden glans and giving a satisfied smile, used the wooden yard to mimic an erection. Now, though, she frowned very deeply, and slowly allowed the yard to decline until it pointed from her pubis downward. Setting the cunny aside and glancing crossly in my direction she used her free hand to work the wooden member, to gesture to it and beckon it as if imploring it to rise, occasionally lifting it a few degrees and dropping it again.

Summer, also in the background, had placed a hand over her own mouth to stifle her amusement, and I was hard put to keep my face straight, realising swiftly from the comic pantomime that the little man before me was not able to get his own little man to perform as the big woman wanted.

What, though, was I to do about it?

I gazed, smiling silently, upon the squatting couple for a brief while, giving myself a moment for thought and realising, somewhat to my surprise, that I was actively and commitedly trying to seek a conclusion. I was not asking myself how to escape this situation, as well I might, but was trying to devise some demonstration or invention which might render them assistance.

Both were strangers, so far as I knew, for it was far beyond my capacity to remember all the faces that had lately dipped within my muff, and yet I felt concern, and even liking, for them. How strange this seemed. And beyond them I could see Summer, holding the artificial cunny before her but with a wryly uncertain grimace on her face, clearly as unsure as I was what the best means of progress might be, whilst June herself was out of my sight, doing I knew not what.

The three of us sat, however, very much as I had sat with Gorrogo, and the shining dark eyes in the homely, pleasant face of the small man had quickly fixed upon the same pink cleft as had Gorrogo's and remained so. And yes, I saw, his questionable manhood was already responding. I knew, then, what I must do.

I rose and stepped forward toward the man, brushed his nose

with my golden bush, placed my hand beneath his chin and gently coaxed him upward, seeing a warmth of hope brighten his good lady's eyes. Small as he was I held him briefly to me, and sensing in him his own great uncertainty I used one hand to press one teat towards his lips. His eyes alight, his arms still straight by his side, he thus began to suckle upon me, gently yet hungrily, and in the observed strangeness of the situation I felt my own loins warming, my nipples hardening.

After feeding him the second teat for a moment or two, I stepped back, to his clear disappointment, but then drew him forward with my hand on his arm and indicated that he should lie down. Foolishly he did so face forward, which had not been my intent, but it took the slightest effort only to coax him over, facing upward.

Madam's eyes were fixed, I saw, upon her husband's member, already achieving greater elevation, I would surmise, than it had ventured for some time, yet not, I thought, sufficient. The bright hope in the lady's eyes, however, supported me in what I had decided with some starting reluctance to undertake, and I positioned myself above him just as I had Minnarra, lowered my cunny to his face.

This odd little man, the stranger between my thighs, now proved so extraordinary an adept with his tongue that I hungered for a way to tell his mistress that she was deeply preoccupied with much the wrong end of him, though I would wonder if she could quite do as I was doing without putting him at risk of suffocation. The tongue I had not seen seemed long and slender, danced a dervish everywhere that set me tingling to my toes and set my clit afire.

More importantly, perhaps—and at least for them—the little man's own little man was now no longer little and, though slender, was hard, erect and long.

Sensing perhaps what I intended, Summer intervened in a way which first surprised me, taking the tip of him gently between her teeth and licking him moistly before anointing him with an unguent of her own provision or perhaps from Gorrogo's stock. The result of combining his juices with mine in the sweating heat-room between my legs, and of Summer's liquid intervention, was to set the body beneath me writhing, the lovely slender cock dark-purpling and straining.

At my gesture, though looking somewhat disbelieving, and whilst her husband teased and heated my clit by some artifice of tongue for which I would love to have a recipe, the wife came forward, poised herself above him and, somewhat gingerly descending, impaled herself upon his ravenous, gloriously rigid prong.

Watching that bulk descending I admit to an expectation that at any moment the crush on his loins might blast my own engorgement with the poor man's expiring gasp, or carry my parts away in the dying clench of moribund teeth. Neither, though, happened, for she had that necessary gift of holding herself and so-distributing her weight as I know makes largeness no impediment to good fucking, and his tongue continued lapping and darting with renewed and enchanting fresh fervour.

The wife's eyes grew huge and round and white, the pupils great black pits of longing, and never left my face for a moment as she rode him, surging up and down before me with the astonishing, supple grace of a dolphin riding waves. In those eyes I saw adulation, directed it seemed at me, and gratitude and warmth, and even observing the sweat-wet rolling vast darkness of her, the boulder-sized vibrating cushions of her enormous bosoms, watching her rolls of flesh ripple even as thrill after rippling thrill surged moist and electric through that tiniest, grandest, covered pink jewel of me, and all of it sourced from the same scrawny male, I lost all desire to find it amusing, all sense of the ridiculous appearance we must have presented.

Wave after wave of wet heat pulsating, rolling upward and outward from the thrill of my clitoris, breasts aching with longing, I could feel myself building, mad-drunkenly climbing to the flood at the top of the hill, and she was gasping, was screaming, wept a terror of pleasure, sweat-wetly bouncing to the thrust, his arse bucking, as he suddenly filled her with moistness of mine, his volcano erupting, and I, I was flying, but hanging suspended in air and in wanting.

She collapsed on bent forearms, still weeping and wet, and liquidly weeping her own and his come on the mat of his groin and his declining manhood, and I felt truly angry, and ready to weep, for the loss, and the emptiness which I must hold secret.

His tongue was still lapping when I arose, he clearly reluctant to give up what he'd had, but he desisted and smiled at me with infinite warmth. And infinite warmth was in her vast, moist embrace, the wet of her tears on my cheeks and my shoulders, the sweat of her body chill on the still-warmth of mine.

Amid a rushing, gushing torrent of words I could not understand, but in tones and expressions which needed no translation, I acknowledged their gratitude as best as I could and watched them depart. June bestowing a small flask upon him of something she'd contrived from Gorrogo's stock, I was left wondering if the memory of this encounter would be enough to restore the man's vigour or whether, perhaps, they'd come to me and with me again.

Neither knowing, nor caring, but weary and aching, my calf-muscles cramped from the effort of kneeling, my neck and my shoulders knotted and stretching as if made of cordage, all suppleness gone, I felt the cold wetness, sticky beneath me and in sudden anger there was a knot in my belly that only a scream could untie.

I stood, then, shivering, aching, burning, like the hapless victim of an ague, and angrily weeping with the hurt of my wanting and the wish not to want so, for it tainted my giving. I was not not-glad to have given. I was not not-happy to have aided, though at that moment I did so dread further asking. I was full, I was empty, and lonely.

Only now something was happening. So many years later the images remain etched upon my mind:

June and Summer are in the doorway, half-silhouetted against a still-bright light of afternoon that gilds the brown glory of their curves and shines in their hair, and they are speaking more unknown words but in tones fully eloquent of authority. Beyond them a knot of waiting people is dispersing and, between the girls and those departing, the guards are now standing not less than three strides from the door. One of the guards argues briefly with Summer, but I perceive that they argue without any heat, and he bows to her persistence and stays where she's posted him.

Their faces quiet, serious, yet still gently smiling, the girls return and June comes toward me and gestures me down to the bed. Some anger remains and I'm fit to refuse her, would quite like to strike her, but can't, and the silent entreaty pleading so lovingly out of those warm brown eyes does suborn me and heavily, angrily, I lie myself down.

And they're at their damned washing and for a moment I hate it, but so quickly that moment is gone. Could you but see the eyes that hover o'er mine as Summer so softly caresses wet-heat from my face, tracing my lips and my obliging eyelids, or could you but feel that so-gentle stroking of wet sponge on nipple and under the breast, curving so sweetly across my curved belly, descending so softly into my valley.

So gently they turn me and wash me anew, cool from the neck, soft down the spine, moistly, firmly moulding cheeks of my bottom. And now there is softness, a soft oily wetness, and the touch of firm fingers from two pairs of hands, probing and kneading, pushing and drawing, slackening cordage, wind-filling my sails and sending me floating.

So very warm, now, and drifting as if on the calmest sea, floating as if on a soft breath of air, and they turn me again. I open my eyes, feeling soft, now, and cosy, and there is the face of my long lovely girl, and two darkest eyes that have never been painted, their black centres vast, warm, dark, welcoming pools, and I see her descending, see her lips for the first time for the perfect little sculptures that they are.

They touch mine.

Can this be?

Could it be otherwise?

The exquisite fullness of her red-brown lips on mine, exquisite pressure of her thighs about my chest, softness of her mound and lips upon the silkiness of my belly, and she takes the arms that might protest and draws them round her to her hind-ward cheeks, silken curves filling soft palms of my hand, moulding to the pressure of my fingers.

Her lips but scarcely moistened I feel moisture new upon the wakeful, fluttering lips below as June gently parts my legs, strokes my inner thighs with satin caresses of her cheeks and dips, tongue moist, toward the needful centre of my being.

I open my lips to moan but hear the sound inside myself alone, my breath and outer sound entrapped in the sweet open chasm of Summer's mouth, my tongue twixt the whiteness of her teeth finding the tongue of hers, tasting hers, trysting wet-softly.

And a fear is come within me, for these sensations are not new, and I know the heat is spreading, carrying me far up on the hill, as June wreaks moist magic and warm havoc upon the silken bud within the flower of me that opens as to the sun. I am climbing again—not climbing, being borne—irresistibly sweeping upward to the storm that prickles in the short fine hair of me, makes lead shot of my teats, flashes, now, and sparkles in me like lightning felt afar, thunders in the whirlwind in my groin.

But I cannot resist them, my need cannot resist them, and as Summer draws her mouth away to breathe I draw her chocolate nipple in, squirming and wetting in the firm, soft, gentle flesh of her, squeezing tight and drawing hard on the round cheeks of her lovely arse, wanting to consume her, and squirming too to an entirely new and magical sensation. For June herself is in me—three, perhaps, of her slender fingers probing inside me, reaching and stroking within my wetness as one gifted finger of her other hand tickles and dances my moist and glistening bud.

I am standing on the very brink, spread-eagle on the mountain crest, my head tilted back, arms and legs outstretched, in face of a raging wind and safe entire, almost. And at that exquisite moment, so often achingly near, so often brutally gone, mislaid by accident of body, I feel the thrusting, and I know what it is, and I know where it is, and it's hard and feels as leather, oiled, and it pushes, and dances, dances and pushes, moves with a celerity scarce attainable by man, and it rubs, and it presses, warming with friction and in my own juices, and Summer is on me, her bubbies warm pressing, her teats jousting steely with mine, her perfect soft mound on my own, while June is still thrusting, my toes twixt her soft lips, and I am now gushing and…

Shuddering, juddering, the Talisman on her reef, I scream before sinking in my too-perfect joy, and screaming I'm drowning, but not within water, for Summer has swallowed the sound that none but my Sam ever heard.

Her gentle hand on my mouth, now, and two faces, side by side, of my two lovely girls, my two lovely lovers, who have taken but joy in my freedom. Tears in their eyes, and tears, yes, in mine, and a rush now of kissing, and petting, and gentling, and a sleep such as I never have known.

Chapter the Fifth

In which a blessed warrior encounters a musical delight.

After so deliciously attending to me, my lovely girls were watching me when I later opened my eyes, but were not now watching from afar. Instead, I woke entwined in their arms, soft-pressed between their warm, firm bodies.

Summer and June appeared to have been awaiting my wakening, for they both now arose, gently disentangling their lovely bodies from mine, and I lay back, warm and languid, watched them wash each other, then suffered them to wash me as they wished. Not once, though, did I take my gaze from them, so smiling and soft, their faces, their eyes, their mouths, and loving me as I was never loved by anyone. I felt sure I needed fear no more, now, that I could offer everything that might be asked of me, and that my girls would love me better, ease my wanting.

Nor was our new, sweet gentle intimacy to be disturbed again, the remainder of that beautiful day.

On the following morn I was much surprised, waking soft and comfortable in Summer's arms, to find our disparate beds moulded into a single one in the centre of the room. Who could help, I wondered, but suspect?

All the utensils of my new-found trade, particularly the oils and the wood-and-leather cock, being restored to their former places, there was nothing but the combination of beds to suggest that aught was changed — yet to one accustomed to English sensibilities that very change spoke scandalous volumes. But this was not England, and I was to happily discover that the combination of beds in such circumstances had caused comment only in that it had not begun on my first waking, for the custom among the people was that all who shared a house would share their beds as well.

Our good-sized home was a one-room dwelling, and so, in fact, were the rest. Since cooking, always, and eating, often, were undertaken out of doors—under the thatched awnings when it rained—and bowel and bladder functions performed by most at goodly distance and beneath the shelter of trees, the houses needed no other rooms save one in which to eat occasionally, to socialise and shelter. Nor did men and women in want of any clothing naturally tend towards prudishness or modesty. There was—save in mine and the two other instances—no question of knocking upon doors, or of any other form of self-announcement.

In consequence, later, about my first forays into the village, I was sometimes caused an embarrassment that I must stifle when visits to another house brought me in sight of lovers fucking, who often paused in the act only long enough to invite me to make myself at home, or when I was brought in sight, whilst walking, of people frankly and openly attending to all the calls of nature.

However, I proceed ahead of myself.

Our first visitor—and first surprise—on the second day really quite alarmed me, being a small, brusque, well-made, but not unpleasant gentleman who came displaying a number of lengths of twine, a wooden tray of damp sand and no indication whatever that he sought my ministrations. Indeed though he seemed always respectful—at such times, anyway, as he forgot his preoccupations long enough to recollect my being there —I sensed I quite annoyed him at times for my lack of understanding, my incomprehension somehow incomprehensible to him, almost as if it were to him just another irritating and inconvenient foible of tiresome womankind.

I could see straightway that he was measuring, though I had no idea for what, and was rather perplexed when his first measurement, taken after I had been cajoled by him and a smirking Summer and June into a standing, legs-apart position, seemed to consist of the distance twixt my cunny and the floor. And he was most precise and exact in this, so that I found myself standing for no little time with my feet a half stride apart, his perspiring head some inches from my quim and his thumb, forefinger and the end of a length of measuring twine reposing, apparently forgotten, a good finger's depth into my cleft. Having established this measurement to his satisfaction and made some marks with a stylus in the sand tray he did much as I have seen others of a similar profession do, wandering about the room with an air of studied perplexity, stretching his measuring strings in various angles and directions, scratching his head or his upper buttock-cleft from time to time, and then scratching out many of the notes he had commenced with.

Before he departed I made a great point of drawing the girls' attention as best I could to the tray of sand, which had given me an idea. But how—without words—to make it clear to them that I required one? I need not have worried. In this, as in so very many things, they proved almost supernaturally intuitive, and a sand-tray reposed among all our other 'business' tools even before our first supplicant, though not our second surprise, arrived.

That second surprise, which almost carried away our curtain, was the delivery into the house—not without sweat and exertion on the part of the half dozen gentlemen who bore it—of the throne which until then had sat outside, like the others, on the common ground. Testimony to that exertion, I thought, was provided by the fact that each of the villagers—all strong men—remained stooped and hunch-shouldered even after they had deposited the throne facing the door with our bed lying almost at its feet. Sensing that for whatever reason the throne was for me I began to move towards it, but found myself gently restrained by the girls until the six stooped gentlemen had left, whereupon I found myself ushered into the new seat with some excitement.

I did not know, but had surmised, that chairs were not the fashion, none having been removed during Gorrogo's expulsion, none remaining, and given the alacrity and facility with which everyone—my girls and visitors—had sat upon the floor. Quite why the throne should have been brought here, then, was a puzzle to me, unless, of course, it was a matter of status. In this I proved truer than I knew.

Our first supplicant that day was an unusually tall and rather handsome young warrior with skin like polished walnut. That considerable stature to which I have referred, however, was not, at first glance, as easy to discern as it might have been. For as June, this time, drew the curtain back, the warrior made entry to our room by crawling over the threshold and across the floor upon his hands and knees, proceeding thus to the bed before me, then manoeuvring himself, without ever straightening, into a seated posture. I could see the girls were much amused by this astounding rigmarole, but could establish no means to find out its purpose.

On his taking his seat certain things became abundantly clear—his imposing stature, his impressive musculature, and the formality of his bearing— and the unquestionable amplitude of his member was quite beyond my missing. What was most un-clear, indeed, was the purpose of his visit, for never could any man—I am sure—appear less in need of virile enhancement.

Taking up a stance behind him, yet clearly in my sight, the girls began their pantomime again, whilst the handsome youth remained gazing at me with obvious interest and curiosity. And I will admit that whilst the throne made it comfortable for me to sit with my thighs together now, and only a little suspecting that his problem might be of erection (his member—soft-inflated on his arrival—was, after all, already pointing toward my feet and rising), I made it my business to part my thighs enough that he might glimpse 'her' nicely.

I quickly divined that erection was not his problem, for in a matter of moments all three of his eyes were rigidly fixated upon my cunny, who was herself swelling gently proud in response to his fascinated attention. Behind him, meanwhile, the smiling girls had already played out the scheme, using my wonderful wooden phallus and another of our many little cups.

No less willing to assist him than I had been the couple the day before, by any means within my power, I regret that I must admit that the culmination of their charming mime somewhat discommoded me. I knew, somehow, to conceal my feelings, and after sitting smiling—in every sense—upon him for several minutes, I rose from my seat and began to pace as if I were deep in thought. And indeed I was, till inspiration hit me.

Pointing toward June and then toward the boy I indicated that she should show him some attention, confident, somehow, that as a 'goddess' I must have such freedom, then I turned my back on both, very conscious of his wistful gaze upon my arse, and proceeded to Alfred's stock.

Within it I had found an object of little value to me but of magical esteem to the girls. This was an ornamented music box, rectangular in shape and decorated with inlaid tortoiseshell and silver filigree. Upon a silver escutcheon on the lid were engraved initials clearly related to those on the pistol and vanity cases, and the object, lined throughout with scarlet velvet, could be nothing but a lady's jewellery container. Immediately beneath the lid lay a shallow tray divided into some five velvet-lined compartments and when this was removed it left but a single, good-sized compartment within.

My back towards the girls and the waiting warrior and having acquired the box, unopened, keeping it carefully out of sight, I proceeded, most discreetly, to acquire two of our little cups — of which we had many, and almost all of them quite identical. Then, after a moment's reflection, and keeping my actions hidden still, I topped one of the cups up with whiskey — whiskey being what I had the most of and what I valued least. Prohibiting the production of music by holding fast the winding key and still keeping the box carefully out of sight, I now removed the little tray and installed the cup of whiskey in its stead, before bearing both the empty cup and the music box reverentially toward my throne.

Well-pleased with the mystified glances of the other three I placed the box beside the throne, and the empty cup upon the arm of the same, and beckoned the young man forward.

His member hard and lovely and clean — I already suspected from observation and participation that all here bathed every day and sometimes several times in a day — I was sorely tempted to sink to my knees and begin its milking with my mouth, but I forbore, not least because on my regaining my seat June and

Summer made clear signs to me that I should stay there.

I therefore took, as it were, the matter in hand, and lovely matter it was too, hard and brown, purple ribbed, and really quite exquisitely beautiful.

A wondrous powerful sensation, was this—the young, virile man squatting on the ground before me, vassal and subject to me, supplicant and dependent upon me, hopeful of my good graces—whilst I leaned forward, full, hard-nippled breasts swinging almost to his face, my cheek almost level with his own, curls of mine bright gold against the deep bronze of his shoulder. The scent of him, too, rising, of the coconut oil I came to love, the light masculine sweat of his stream-washed body and that other warm odour too which might, at that moment, have been his or mine.

I drank it in as I would have drunk him in if I could, in all his dark, muscled strength, his lithe, athletic splendour. This is what the name Adonis means, I realised. Youths such as this wore scant armour about their warrior nakedness in the battlefield before Troy, or as they contested upon the fields of Olympus. It was glorious.

But for the colour, my warrior's appendage put me much in mind of my lovely Sam's, and save that I did not attempt—elevation, distance and my girls' manners indicating to the contrary—to suck him, I gave him everything my hands, wrists and fingers had to give. And, as Sam would attest, that was no little, for I had been his most eager student both in giving and receiving. I had early learned, therefore, the difference betwixt a man's cock and a fire-pump, that 'tis not a matter of mere up and down, but of playing and plying, of twisting motions of the hand and fluid caresses, of a palm floating up and over and around the helm, slinking silkily around and under the ridge of it, drawing it back, coaxing it forth, till the dewdrop comes, glistening, the gleam of a smile in the eye of a cock.

Even had I not possessed such skills the young man might scarce have felt the lack, for both the girls assisted, to his joy, massaging his thighs and lower belly, anointing my hand and his member in unison with fragrant oils from a flask, now and again cradling and teasing his balls.

Not long, then, ere his eyes showed a tendency to roll, the muscles of his face to succumb to that wondrous St Vitus' Dance twixt pain and exultation that betokens the cock and the need taking control, as it seems, of all. Not too long, though we did not hurry it, ere the girls were supporting him as he began to totter in extremis, and I, gauging the moment as was needed, tipped and milked him into the empty cup.

Still warm, palely milky, I might have jolted it back, if that would have served the purpose, for it did look quite delightful. But I had learned from the mime that that would not serve, however, and I was about to participate, had I but known it, in the one particular ritual Gorrogo was most happy to be relieved of, and which was the once-in-a-lifetime mark of a warrior's graduation to full status. Had I but known the latter—that the youth knew no more of exactly what would follow and how than I did—I might have been spared some agony of indecision. But I knew not, on that first occasion, what the warrior knew, and how transparent or otherwise would prove my ploys.

June and Summer, however, had mimed the mutual, lengthy, alternate sipping at their cup of imagined semen with a patent relish I was not at all sure that I would share. Fresh and warm with the heat of passion or simple delight is one thing, but now, decanted into a cup and cooling faster than my own ardour, I was not at all sure of acquiring the taste or accommodating the texture, and thus I took the greatest risk—as I then thought—that I had taken since my arrival on the island.

Watching the warrior as he recovered and as the girls lifted him up off his arse and eased him onto his knees, I saw his gaze fall upon the brimming cup and as I raised the small vessel, just as it passed his face, I felt sure I saw a shudder there. I realised that however much he might repress his feelings he was no more enamoured of what was to come than I was. This, I know, helped me.

Holding the cup aloft I kissed it first and gestured to Summer to pass me the box, counting that she would lift it as she previously had, and, indeed, in the manner in which I had delivered it, reverentially and in both hands, therefore keeping it approximately level and not undoing my plan. When the box was safely thus conducted and sat upon my knee I kissed the cup a second time, gestured to the boy to do the same, holding the rim above reach of his lips, and I opened the lovely wooden casket.

Even foreknowledge could not protect my senses from the seemingly ghastly incongruity of the popular Germanic march that tinkled from within, but I was glad to see that my miniature congregation were simply mesmerised. Carefully, with all the appearance of reverence that I could muster, and screening my actions behind the raised casket lid, I placed the second cup alongside the first, already inside the box. Both cups hidden from observation, I sealed it. Now I closed my eyes, began to murmur the first piece of doggerel which entered my head (Mary, Mary, Quite Contrary, if I now remember correctly) as if it were an incantation, and swept my hand dramatically around the surface of the case several times.

About to cheat I dared not cheat entirely, and opening the box to the same awful melody again, still screening my actions behind the upright lid, I discreetly tipped but a drop or two of his into the cupful of mine before placing his within. Then I lifted my own identical cup, only un-identical in content, carefully from the music box, closed the lid as I did so, and returned the casket to Summer.

Lifting my eyes to Heaven, but praying only to Fortune, I raised the cup very slowly and, as was my due, sipped it first. Catching but a little of mixture where the film of his juice floated on top, I sipped mostly whiskey and fire, and found it not, in the circumstances, overly unpalatable. I disclosed to the others, however, not the slightest reaction, for though whiskey was never my tipple of choice I have long been inured to alcohol's bite, and I passed the small vessel to the youth.

He looked as if he would fain hold his nose and clearly wanted not to look, though he did not the first but did the second, and it was at that moment that I knew my greatest alarm. His senses of sight and smell, unless much affected by his milking, could not but know that what they now encountered was not what he had given. What I counted upon, of course, was magic, that believing me capable of any transformation, and having had no chance to encounter whiskey before; he would assume the difference was of my making. He did.

Never, though, have I seen anyone look quite so stricken as he at that first imbibing, and I—beginning to enjoy myself, happy to have spared myself and him—made a show of sipping subsequently that was almost entirely show, so that at the end of the lengthy business the generous shot of Highland dew was almost entirely his.

Unsurprisingly for someone who had not previously experienced Scotland's amber delight, the young man departed much happier than he might have done, if unsteadier yet on his hands and knees. There dawned upon me a suspicion, of course, that fairly soon there might be any number of younger warriors seeking to attain whatever this blessing—not then understood by me—betokened.

Almost as the doorway curtain fell behind his retreating, and somewhat swaying arse I heard the jangling of that dreadful music and turned, stunned and afraid.

Summer was holding the sperm cup and gazing directly at me, her expression both rueful and—it seemed to me—amused. 'Twas she removed it, and I never heard another word.

We saw no-one else that day, which was puzzling, for I recollected the small waiting queue of the previous day and was sure that I had heard and glimpsed a similar phenomenon earlier in the morning. I might well have been somewhat alarmed at this sudden arrest in the chain of events had not Summer and June stayed so brilliant and cheerful and obviously happy with me, keeping me occupied in so many small ways.

One of these was the sand tray and stylus. Having found great efficacy in their wondrous abilities with pantomime there were still many questions which, wordless, were beyond me, and having developed a lady's facility in drawing I was keen to experiment on the curious 'slate'.

Within perhaps an hour of my first ever awakening upon the island and finding myself so intimately attended by these two lovely girls I had sought to apprehend their names. It is I think a normal reflection of the human need for companionship. And the girls had swiftly responded, in sound and gesture, with the names I interpreted as Summer and June. For me, however, they already had a name, or a title—I knew not then what it meant—and I had some difficulty, until the sand tray came to my hand, convincing them that there was another name that I preferred. And even so I was to err, as you will see, even if rather delightfully.

By way of introduction I drew some of what had happened, using crude, simple pictures and symbols. I drew an outline figure, indicated its masculinity with the outline of a penis, and choosing the principal means of his outward identification sketched a very tall feather at the figure's head. June murmured some words in response, of which one she repeated was 'Arshon'. Drawing another outline beside it, adding round tits, a sharp 'vee' at the groin with a cunny-slit marked up the centre, and a bushy feather to one side of the head, produced a definite 'Minnarra', repeated nodding, and 'Arshon!' spoken firmly with a finger pointing at the man. Thus, with some little practice, did I learn the names or the titles—I could not be sure which—of our king and his lady.

Scrubbing away the pictures—to their no small dismay—I redrew the queen in a supine position, the figure in profile, and they nodded assent when I pointed to her and said: "Minnarra?" Now, then, I drew myself in profile, as sitting over her face. The girls giggled hugely and offered a number of words which I could not quite tie down to firm meaning. Possessed of a fresh idea I pointed at the image of myself, pointed directly at myself and began: "Me, Lady (but thinking better of the title added)... Susanna," which sounds they delightfully repeated very accurately within but few attempts. Unfortunately, however, I was lost then to find a way of removing the personal pronoun and title I had unwittingly introduced, no matter that I tried, and for long afterwards was known to both of them most often as either 'Me Lady Susanna' or more frequently 'Me Lady', accidentally re-endowing myself with a form of address I had not intended. 'Me Lady', however, sounded so beautiful when they used it that I soon came to accept it.

To the drawing of myself kneeling above the lovely queen's face I added the angled body of the king, his exaggerated member tilting at his lady's outline cunny, and I shivered warmly at the memory of my body engaging both their tongues as he kissed her through me, fucked me through her. The girls found the image as gently amusing as I found it warmly distracting, and they produced in response a number of words which again were hard to ascribe.

Starting again clean, to their clear disappointment, forgotten the moment I began afresh to draw, I drew—larger and in some detail—an image of our common private parts. Already long-acquainted with the form of the masculine cock I found myself drawing the female appendage with a greater ease and efficacy than I might ever previously have known, and found myself, too, dwelling long upon the small and intimate details to which for almost all my life I had been a stranger. And in doing so, of course, I could not but be reminded of the means by which I had latterly become so well acquainted with the sweet topography of the cunny—the soft-inflating lips, the nestling inner petals and the glistening bud which I had for the first time seen at such close quarters within but the last few hours.

For the cunny, now, I seemed to have a name, and discovered—to my no great surprise—that the same word formed a part of the title by which they had previously addressed me. It would be some time before I would learn the full translation and discover with considerable embarrassment that I was commonly referred to as 'She of the Golden Mother Chasm which is the Gateway to Heaven' or, from time to time, simply as 'Golden Mother'.

A penis drawn separately easily provided their word for that,

whilst drawing the male and female parts conjoined and rein-
forcing my intent by taking the wooden yard and sliding it into
the bowl vagina seemed to produce their lovely words for fucking.

Now, determined, and far less self-consciously than ever I
could have imagined, I gently wrested the simulated cock from
Summer's grip, and gripping it with both hands so that the tip
pointed toward me, lowered it slowly toward my groin. A knot
in my belly at thus performing before my two girls and moist
within, both for the same reason and on account of the memories
recently wakened, I slid the polished helmet gently and slowly
within me and using their word asked "Fucking?"

Summer responded somewhat hesitantly with one of the
few English words I had sought, then, to teach them, answering;
"Yes?" It left me unsatisfied. I could not know if her questioning
tone might indicate her uncertainty with the yet scarcely practiced word, or might be a qualification of her answer, so that it
might refer specifically to the wooden cock. Wooden cocks, to
be truthful, were not then my principal preoccupation and the
answer was insufficiently clear. I now carefully, therefore, drew
a supine body, and after adding the necessary details, began,
pointing; "Me…"

Both girls nodded quickly, responding "Me Lady" and flashing me most delightful smiles, and I taking that as close enough
identification rather reluctantly withdrew the wooden cock and
set it aside, then drew in the sand a male figure, his organ buried
almost to the hilt in mine. This, to be truthful, produced a look
of shock and horror which would not have seemed out of place
among any gathering of maiden aunts in an English drawing
room, and when I then combined their words and mine to produce "Fucking Me Lady" I was met with tightened lips, firmly
shaken heads and that other English word which always seems
to be the first we learn; 'No!'

It was, it seemed, as I had feared.

Only now Summer took the stylus from me and added some
marks of her own around the member. Seeing I failed to under-

stand, she moved over to Gorrogo's gifts and returned. Inserting the handle of the wooden cock beneath her mound (and oh how I envied that wooden haft!) and making the pantomime we knew to mean a man—back straight, chest out, cock up—she drew over the wooden phallus the diaphanous sheath of animal skin (confirming the purpose I had previously guessed, having once encountered something similar in a tryst with a certain European gentleman) and tied it in place with a bow of twine. Then she said:

"Fucking Me Lady, Yes!"

Cocks I could have inside me. Living seed I could not. Or could I?

Carefully I scratched out an image of feminine lips, a tongue and open mouth, opened my own and pointed to it. The girls nodded. I now drew an inflated penis—and rather well, being so well acquainted with them—drawing its tip on 'my' illustrated tongue. Summer and June were now watching with anticipation, making signs neither of approval or otherwise but smiling enough at the image and venturing words which might or might not have referred to fellatio. With careful erasure, then, I modified and re-drew the mouth, closed about the shaft, and Summer clapped her hands together.

"Me Lady?" I ventured, pointing at the picture.

"Yes, yes! Me Lady yes!" I heard, accompanied by vigorous nodding.

Fellatio, then, I could have, but sex—other than with this uncommon intervention of the sheath of skin—was not permitted me. It was a mystery to me and a cause of much early chagrin but it would, in time, be explained to me.

My lovely, naked, brown friends, you see, whatever they might have lacked in the way of libraries and theatres, universities and colleges, possessed a wonderful intelligence. They knew that despite their own broad perceptions to the contrary and an abhorrence of the idea of anyone being 'owned' by anyone else, there remained in some individuals—female and male—a sense that penetration implied possession, especially and most particularly if that 'possession' produced a child who would, in some sense, be somebody's heir.

It was unseemly, to them, that a mortal man should attempt to father a child with a goddess or with that goddess's representative. And it was perceived, too, that the fathering of a child to someone whose duty was to love many would, for one thing, incommode her for a period of time and would, more importantly, lead to antagonisms among men who would seek to establish higher-than-mortal status by claiming the child as of their making.

It was a wisdom I was long in ignorance of, though I could not but witness its effect upon me and my too-often yearning body. I would wonder, betimes, if I would ever know a real and naked cock between my thighs again.

Certainly at that moment, my cunny moist with memory and reflection and almost audibly panting, it seemed to me, for the return of the wooden phallus at least, the prospect of even such protected sex produced in me a hunger that quite hurt, but who was to provide it?

Could I exit our cabin, perhaps, grab the nearest swarthy guard by his cock and drag him in to do me service? Given the intimacy we had already known, my own definite attraction toward him and the hint of attraction toward me that I was persuading myself I had glimpsed in his expression, might I stroll across the way and fetch Arshon from his wife to do the same, always assuming the protective sheath would actually fit around the astonishing engorgement I had already witnessed? Of course, I did not know. And how, with a tray of sand as an implement, was I to pose the question?

Perhaps I could have found a way then, perhaps I should have, but the prospect somehow defeated me, and anyway the girls were pressing other matters upon me, eager to utilise the sand-tray in order to communicate something to me.

Using small drawings of quite exquisite subtlety—as if both had been drawing throughout their lives—Summer and June drew representations of myself in various postures—standing, kneeling, sitting and so forth—then coupled those with sketches of other people, represented as being in my presence. Whenever such a figure was shown with their head at an elevation equal to or higher than my own, both girls enunciated a resounding and frequently repeated 'No' with much exaggerated shaking of heads and wagging of fingers. In whatever situations, however, the people in the drawings were represented to me as having their heads lower than my own, they produced an equally resounding 'yes', accompanied by a no-less vigorous nodding. I began, I thought, to understand.

Someone, almost certainly Arshon, had decided as a matter of status that no-one should be placed in a position from which they could physically gaze down upon me. Bearing in mind our own vocabulary and the phrase 'to look down upon' as meaning to despise, I could see a certain rationality in the idea. Being taller than the majority of the native people it would seem to pose little problem for me, either, but I could see how it might affect the perception of some of my ministrations. I had bowed, after all, to kiss Gorrogo's cock, and the mountainous lady of that other encounter had certainly—when rising up with her husband's member—at times been 'taller' than I. And I believed I understood, now, why the throne had been delivered, why its deliverers had remained stooped whilst I had been enjoined to remain standing and why our one latter caller had both entered our chamber and left it, walking on his hands and knees.

Curiosity and interest had for the nonce abated my inner yearnings, but I knew they would not remain thus quiescent for long. Elements of our earlier conversations and my reflections on recent events had repeatedly warmed and stirred me, and came back to me whenever I took repose. To be bathed by them, to feel the often intimate caresses of them as they paid attention to my needs, to be surrounded by this constant warmth of touch and affection, was sometimes exquisite agony. And was it necessary, I wonder, for Nature to embellish these glistening, mahogany sculptures with feminine accoutrements of such bright icing sugar pinkness, such chocolate brown-ness?

On retirement to our conjoined beds I know that it seemed to me that my gilded bush was to my body as a cross is to the treasure map of popular fable and marked 'the spot'—the spot that ached, now, hungered, now, for satisfaction. But how to seek it? Lying gazing up at the ceiling, warmed by the nubile forms of Summer and June beside me and feeling the incidental caress of their skin against mine, I prayed inwardly that they might essay a repetition of the previous day's lovely events but they did not, and were, instead, soon sound asleep. Weary as I was I felt a pang of disappointment, fleetingly cross at this noticeable and unforgivable failure of their often wondrous intuition. Turning onto my comfortable side I felt the sleeping girls' unconscious accommodation, felt them shift till Summer's gently downy mound nuzzled into the cleft of my arse and June, before me, snuggled inward and backward, the soft firm cheeks of her bottom pressing sweetly into my groin.

But a little later Summer stirred softly in her sleep, turned half away and back, this time slipping an unconscious arm about my waist, her fingers light on my belly, hand sliding down until it rested, prevented from further descent—such poignant tantalisation—just where June's flesh pressed softly on my own. So torn, then! Should I pull away, just a tiny little, in hope that that resting hand would slide and glide the little further until it reposed upon the junction of my legs? And could I achieve that, feeling those fingers so close, could I bear it, or must I lie the night awake hoping they will be drawn to the radiating warmth and moistness just beneath?

A little angry at myself, a little angry at my life, I steeled myself, placed my own arm round the sleeping June, gently caressed the curve of her abdomen, rested my hand on the warmth of her mound.

I so wished, then, to wake her, to continue, hand sliding, till my fingers nestled within her, but I knew not the rules as yet. Yesterday I had been their passive love object and gave them joy in being so. I could not know that my becoming active, initiating an encounter, would not offend them, and in this poignant, wondering state of mind, I drifted slowly into sleep, little suspecting the efforts even then proceeding to confirm me in my rather special status, nor what the consequences would be.

Chapter the Sixth

*In which an English Milady is raised
to heights altogether new.*

I was awoken to breakfast the following morning, waking
with Summer lying at my back, arm over me, gently trawl-
ing her fingers through my golden pubic curls. June was
standing smiling at me with our breakfast platter in hand and
the morning sun beamed cheerfully through the doorway, our
curtain temporarily tied back. Lying with the intelligent Summer thus, and quite uncovered, I knew we were visible to anyone
passing and knew, therefore, that her action was proper, that no-
one considered it wrong. That cheered me, as did our morning
three-way embrace and our ever-delightful breakfast. I still rather knew not what we were eating, for the most part, but it clearly
agreed with my system; I was entirely regular already and felt
better than I could ever remember.

Regularity of bowel, of course, compelled me to submit to
the one service of theirs which seemed, at first, to most deeply
threaten what little remaining dignity I might have pretended
to.

Scarcely was breakfast over when a guard appeared at the
open doorway and rapped, somewhat unnecessarily in the circumstances, sharply upon the doorpost. Summer attended to his
enquiry, almost skipping to the door, and immediately afterwards
our head-scratching, measuring, note-taker appeared—followed
rather alarmingly by a small gang of men. Bearing in mind our
previous 'conversation in the sand' I made sure that I was standing and was not overlooked.

Trusting to June and Summer's management I simply stood
back, watched as the head-scratching foreman coaxed my throne
to one side and observed with some astonishment as the men
from the labour gang struggled somewhat to introduce a new
item of furniture.

Whatever 'twas, it was delivered in pieces, a strange timber puzzle which the foreman began to decipher, handing part-assembled sections and bits to his underlings, positioning them thus and thus, muttering and cajoling men and parts into agreement. And then there was the slotting together, the marriage of parts and a mallet and banging of carefully carved pegs into carefully shaped holes, and the whole affair was standing, a mystery.

In essence a chair and not un-like the throne, its most visible surfaces intricately carved, the seat was much higher and only reached by a step. At the forefront of the chair seat, though, was a cutaway hole, its rim edges carefully rounded, and the wood around it artfully moulded to form a proportionately wide and shallow basin.

Beginning to form a glimmer of its purpose, even as all but its designer departed, I had to expend quite some effort in holding back my laughter and sheer perverse delight.

Somewhat grand, remarkably crafted in so short a space of time with implements which one knows must be primitive by European standards, the workmanlike device represented a seat which, were the sitting platform itself of normal construction, would have placed my buttocks and my quim around the level of the eyes of an average man. Owing to the cavity in the seat there, however, designed to embrace and support my thighs and a proportion of my arse, my cunny, some measure of my hind cheeks and that other most vulnerable aperture of my bottom could not but hang suspended through that embrasure, open, vulnerable and designedly approachable.

Beneath the seat cavity, moreover, and beneath the space into which my treasured cunny would hang suspended, there sat, of all things, a wooden bench. Efficiently hinged about its middle, the end of the bench nearest the seat could be raised and lowered by the adjustment of ropes, lifting the head of any supplicant upon it up towards that space wherein my very maidenhood would repose. At the same time their own upper body would recline, comfortably supported, on the hinged portion of the bench upon which they lay.

I was both amused and quietly much impressed by the craft which had gone into this rather lovely, articulated cunny-kisser, and she herself was tingling, softly trembling with anticipation, as I inspected the contrivance with interest.

Chair, ramp and bench, I saw with some relief, were carefully conjoined at the floor by beams and cross-spars which made the whole enterprise stable, if not very portable. And I was truly quite pleased when my head-scratching little artisan, actually beaming as he bowed, most politely, gestured to me to try it.

Who could not but have felt foolish, in this workmanlike setting, finding themselves seated stark naked and at that strange elevation? I already understood its purpose and its meaning, however, and I somehow understood that its maker, wanting to know that he had served me well and seeking justification for his natural pride, stood, as yet, in need of reassurance. And thus I sat, my arms, back, buttocks, thighs all quite comfortably supported, my cunny already warming as it projected very visibly, vulnerable, pale, and suspended, through the carefully-modelled aperture.

And still the man was frowning and unsure and—well, why not? Already I had learned, in truth, some of the reality of my status here, and impressed and warmed by the scale of his achievement, and grateful for the pleasure and amusement he seems to have given my two sweet girls in the process, it seemed reasonable to reward him. Reaching down with my hand I touched my fingers to my pinkening flower, raised the same fingers and beckoned him forward. Little June, ever thoughtful, lowered the curtain, Summer bestowed fur blankets on the bench, and, eyes moist at the generosity of my reward, the little man approached. Standing, he was beneath me, and sitting on the bench was even more so. I gestured to June, feeling the ambience somehow wrong, and she floated gently towards him and helped to lift his legs onto the board.

Now seated along the bench, his buttocks and legs supported, he was able to lean gently back, assisted still by June, only to find that in this configuration he was too tall. But the top of the ramp, as I have observed, was supported by stout cords wrapped around strong pegs and before he could bid them do so June and Summer carefully released them, lowered him gently and evenly, raised him a little again, and tied the cords off.

I gazed down from my strange elevation, could see my smiling girls, could witness the increasing elevation and the growing lovely hardness belonging to the man who now lay comfortably beneath me and whose tongue beneath my seat began its work.

I closed my eyes, tilted my own head back, focused on the focus of his tongue and clenched my teeth together even as my arse cheeks clenched themselves, my hands, too, about the arm rests, knuckles whitening.

He emerged wet, and happy, blessed and hugely erect, and walked backward from the room almost weeping. I wondered how he would ease it. Did he have some woman waiting? I hoped so, truly. And I descended from my wondrous love-throne, embraced my girls, enjoyed a cleansing.

I had realised, of course, that the surprising dearth of supplicants for my ministrations had resulted from Arshon's intervention and represented merely a hiatus whilst the issue of my 'elevation' was resolved. I did not expect to wait long before the next petitioners arrived, and indeed my cleansing was barely over before the next rap upon the doorpost sounded.

The new arrivals were a couple who, like Arshon and Minnarra, were striving for a baby and who placed within my hands the self-same carvings as had he. To use my brand new love-throne would not, I knew, quite answer if he was to take her sweetly, and so I stood astride the ramp which lifted her the necessary little upwards to me, whilst her arse rested on the bench-end where he knelt, patiently waiting. And I could watch it all from here, the burgeoning of his manhood, his sliding it within her, his changes of expression and his tension, the thrusting of his loins, the exultant quivering of her hips and thighs, the raising of her knees and the bonding of her legs around him, drawing him into her, beseeching the heat of him, hungry for the gush of him.

Gripping her by her thighs he was thrusting and thrusting,

pushing and giving, rubbing her backward and forward beneath and betwixt me, she all the while suckling my lips and my pearl. But for the girls standing at my elbows I'd have been teetering, my consciousness waning in my own heat and my wanting, and they knew what was coming, Summer's soft palm resting on my mouth, lest it need stifling—and it did. My eyes wide and staring, Summer's hand scent in my nostrils, the heat of her firm palm clamped tight o'er my face, my thighs knew no feeling and on feeble legs I was tottering, my cry echoing within me, for the three of us were coming, and coming as one.

The couple afterwards were so grateful, and if they saw how much I was affected they showed me no sign, she face-wet and streaming with saliva and my flooding and perspiring, he perspiring too and with ribbons of his overflow festooned upon his matt of curly hair. It was not, I learned, our practice to cleanse them. They would go now to their home, I later learned, oiled and sticky with our juices and our perfumes, to lie down in deep embrace and in their hoping, proceeding only later to the stream and gentle bathing.

Their expectation frightened me. I knew I was no deity or spirit, that any gift which lay within my cunny was given too oft to tawdry men, shared too often and too easily in my memory and never ever once as a holy thing. Not even with Sam. Just as I took joy in him, so Sam took joy in me, athletically and with every show of verve, yet every time was as a race we ran, collapsing together at the end, sharing the run, the pace, the glad exhaustion. But Sam the stud was never mine, nor thought me his, nor called me so except in such throes as might have made him swear perpetual love and fidelity to any village doxy, or had he the inclination, to the relieving arse of a sheep. Relief is what it was, and fun, and play, but I never worshipped him, he never worshipped me.

Yet worship was mine then, worship of my worthless, ill-used sheath, my curling blondeness, the accidental whiteness of my flesh, made holy in their wanting. And I did not deserve it, though I sought to, and I could not deserve it as they hoped. No wetting of my cunny with mouth and tongue was going to produce a child for them, and it was surely only time before this came known? What then? How they would hate and despise me!

I would have my failures, could not but have my failures — and, oh, how they would turn upon me then!

I would learn, one day, of my error. I had forgotten, very simply, the simple lessons of my growing, the simple lessons of the religion custom had compelled me to absorb. Seated with my father in the family pew and gazing betimes upon the faces of our inferiors, did I not know how hard and fruitlessly they prayed? Yet still they kept praying, clinging to belief. The two who brought their crook-legged child to the altar, all the years after a heedless carriage had smashed him, who waited and prayed for miraculous straightening and never received it. Yet still they believed. It was not the will of their God, they said, or he had other plans, or they did not deserve it. Such I knew were the rationalisations — and I knew them full well. I had heard my father pray and weep, and had prayed and wept in company with him, when I was but seven years old and mother lay in her childbed, hurting. We prayed for her and for him who would have been my brother Tommy, prayed they would be restored to us. And when both were lost to us, and went at least to a peace we might only dream of, did we not consider our prayers were answered?

So it was to be here. I could not fail. Those who were blessed and prospered considered their fortune my blessing; those who were blessed without the sought-after consequence could always find justification for its absence.

But I did not know this then, and lived in great fear of disclosure. And I had other fears, too.

Equipped with my wonderful love-throne and with a goddess's endless appetites, it seemed as if no-one considered that my fount might ever need cosseting. The cunny, they thought, was the grand panacea, the gateway to Heaven, the exit therefrom, and whilst other faiths taught ascension through blue skies or descents through dark caverns our people thought Heaven a vast, warm wet womb entered by the Earth Mother's slit.

In the very intensity of their passion and wanting, the couple, Heaven bless them, had gifted my coming, but the first joy of wet tongue on clit was fast fading, the memory of June and the woodcock suffusing, overwhelming the need-centred part of my mind. I wanted invasion, and I wanted, too, to invade. I could think of little else.

Others could think, it seemed, of nothing but cunny, and even now they waited, and no doubt for more of the same. My loins were beginning to ache, now, with dread.

It proved not, though, as bad as it might have. The next candidate was a warrior, ascending in rank like his predecessor of the day before. In truth, though I thought of and called them both so, neither were warriors when they stepped through my doorway, only young men who'd completed their fighting apprenticeship, and whose official graduation to warrior status was attained through their visit to me.

My about-to-graduate warrior presented some small difficulty insofar as the question of height was concerned, for, from the love-throne which gave me certainty of at least equal height I could scarcely reach his manly yard, let alone please it, and there seemed no posture adoptable on the bench which would not either have brought his head above mine or placed his member at such an angle that his fluid could never be cupped.

I remained, therefore, standing, until he knelt before me, only then myself sitting down upon the lesser throne and attending to his manhood just as I had his warrior precursor.

Intriguingly, 'twas the very first time in my many similar encounters that one of these young fighting men would present to me quite as he did, barely condescending to look upon me and maintaining at first an arrogant hauteur that put me in mind of the worst of my lovers. 'If I must endure this foolishness', his sharply handsome face both eloquently and silently declaimed; 'then endure it I must, and endure it I will, but, prithee, do not dally!'

A foolish error, methought.

Neither novice nor virgin at such play — though never in such circumstance — I had been a diligent student of the skills no less important, in my view, to ladies, than the ability to read, to draw, to ride a horse, tinkle the clavichord or pluck a melody from a harp. I had taught myself well those parallel skills of how to pleasure a man in pursuit of what I wanted, could read the lineaments of his expression, draw his milk, ride him comfortably, tinkle his purse and pluck from it what was needed.

Whilst it was true that the girls had checked the engorging pulse of the warrior of the day before, and had tipped him and cupped him at the moment most prime, 'tis fact that I could have done as well myself. And having in my nature little time for or patience with arrogant young bastards, and having just been reflecting on the cunny-daunting prospects before me, I resolved to teach this one arrogant young bastard a timely and most salutary lesson.

In first hopes of thawing him I continued warmly smiling, and kept on smiling even when I knew that he would not, gently waved sweet Summer and June away when they drew near to monitor his cock, and played him as my solo instrument. It was to be a virtuoso performance. Hard as he fought against displaying any sign of his burgeoning need it was not very long until I felt it building in the increasing fullness, rigidity and dark suffusion of his manly appendage. Once begun, of course, and with but slight endeavour, I kept him building, building, and building — and then, with a judgement still impeccable — I slowed.

Slow, slow, and very light, my touch. My having brought him to the crest, he slithered slowly, now, back down the hill, and the girls were standing behind him, covering their mouths with their hands and hugging themselves with stifled laughter.

Then hard again, and fast again, backsliding the over-skin of his cock from the stubby, circling ridge of his helmet, sweeping it forward again, and over, so that under the warmth of my eager hand I felt a fresh resurgence, saw sweat upon his brow, his chin, and there was the lovely pulse and...

Slow, slow, slowly again, sliding back down the hill.

I made the bugger squirm, believe me; drew him to the desperate brink at least a half a dozen times and let him, each time, fall away, and he could not complain, was entirely at my godly disposal. At the end of my ministrations the boy was as a shaking leaf, his face contorted worse than fear or pain could write it, in an agony of wanting, his balls big and hard as full-ripe plums and purple as his thickly-corded, monstrous, luscious, aching cock, and I paused again, as I must, and Summer passed me my box and the waiting empty cup.

Ye Gods! My box! As a fist to the stomach, even as I began to lift the lid, I realised I'd not prepared it! And even I was scarce prepared to leave the youth in this state for sufficient time to make my preparations. 'Serves me right!' I thought, for punishing him this way.

Looking at him, dark and huge and purpling, a film of sweat weeping from all points of his body, a suspicion of weeping even, around his barely-focused eyes, the tinkling strains of the music box seemed more incongruous than ever. And he was not mesmerised by it as was his precursor, but seemed not to notice, deaf to it, blind to it, so great was he in wanting.

And I could have wept, almost—I who do not believe in miracles! For my box contained a cup of golden liquid, Heaven-sent and heather-scented, and my two girls were smiling at me. Will they continue to do so when I'm so cruel?

For then I took him in my hand again and fluidly began my work again, drawing and sliding, drawing and sliding, softly palming the juicy purple helmet of his swollen warrior, calling it to strict attention, playing fife and drum in the rhythm of my fingers on his manly yard and balls, sounding the charge and starting the gallop, watching him buck like a man who is dying as muscles in confusion of need and relief now struggled to remember their purpose.

It was not a warrior sound that followed, then, but a weakly gasping, crying moan of a man enfeebled, a shuddering of humours from knees to neck, and I tipped him hard as he exploded whitely, turgid, frothingly over-laden, into the waiting vessel.

In the extreme of his distraction he was so blind to all about him that it would need no subtlety nor sleight of hand from me, having closed the box and stroked its lid as a matter of form, to have offered him his cup alone, both to kiss and sup, and, switching cups in each transaction, to alone imbibe the liquid fire in mine.

I could not do so, poor child, and did as I did before, pretending only to sip, this time, until what was his was gone, and wishing to weep with laughter when the liquid fire first hit his virgin throat and belly and he was coughing and spluttering like one fallen in a midden.

Recalled to himself at last, we betrayed to our warrior no sign of his cuckolding and he found us solicitous and kind, knew nothing of the signals I had flashed to my Summer, the faces I'd pulled, the gestures of exaggeration. But I knew, somehow, that she understood quite everything as I moved to my greater elevation before the youth could stand, suspended my pink inflation within its wooden crown.

I did not know her words, but could read her earnest expressions of awe and amazement, knew she was telling him something akin to what I had sought to suggest to her—of how powerful I had found his magic, how huge was his yard, how great his potency. Which was why, of course, I was offering him what I did not offer the other—my own very special blessing.

He tried very hard, poor weary soul, and kissed and sucked and suckled, the whiskey a little stinging still on the vulnerable skin he tasted. He had not the energy, though, to fetch me where I wished to go, nor even to carry me far.

My girls' mouths were compressed and wry with simulated disapproval; their eyes alight with sparkling merriment, and the embrace we shared when he was gone shuddered with silent laughter. He had gained, after all, everything he had looked for, and a little extra beside, and we, being women, shared a sweet commonality in knowing the bastards men can be and a joy in their come-uppance.

I knew that when next I saw him I would smile the smile I know that floats a man on air, and had no doubt he'd go on being an arrogant bastard, but someone else's, not mine. I could not help feeling I would somehow pay, though, for my breech of solemnity.

There followed an oddity, now, for which I had never bargained. Summer held back the curtain for one of the smallest girls I had yet seen here among them, perhaps of a score years old by her face, though one might have thought her still younger had she not been wearing the modesty thong. Her eyes were downcast and she looked far from happy, whilst in her hand she held a length of twine which trailed behind her, and just as I was wondering what could possibly ail her—unless 'twas a matter of size—the slave appeared.

Looking otherwise no different to any other village man it was clear that something had profoundly and rather mysteriously subdued him, for the twine around his neck was far too insubstantial to stop a grown man breaking free of it and running. Yet here he was, placidly walking behind her, stooped, shoulders hunched by the heavy weight of an object he was carrying for her and which at first glance I supposed he could easily have discarded. Supported of necessity by both of his hands it looked much like—yet surely could not be—a good size cannonball of stone.

It was not. It was his penis. Or at least, his penis was a part of it.

It was a ball, and quite enormous, and was made of some strong form of clay or amalgam embedded, and I would later learn, shot through, with small pebbles, stone chippings and fragmented sea-shells. Save for a slender hole running through its core for him to piss through it was solid-set about his cock and balls and, I would discover, irremovable without the aid of two strong men, a very large hammer, and very great care.

Whilst I was wondering what on earth was afoot my June had proceeded to our long table—a raft of bamboo standing upon simple trestles—which we used to store our increasing supply of equipment and materials. Here, now, reposed a small orgy of carved wooden cocks, fresh supplies—garnered by my girls—of many more of the leaves and powders of which Gorrogo had provided the first, a bowl of dead and mummified small serpents, two wings of a parrot, partly-plucked and a variety of other things besides, most of their uses then as yet unknown to me. Beneath the bamboo board stood another, lower trestle which had served no obvious purpose. It was this which June retrieved, brought forward and placed before me, horizontally across my body and about level with my quim.

Cannon-ball-cock looked up at me from under lowered eyebrows and waddled flat-footedly towards me before turning almost rudely away. There was something in his eyes, I realised, which I had not expected, and suddenly I recognized disdain. Following so soon after our contemptuous warrior this surprised and disturbed me, no less than the abruptness with which he had turned his back on me.

Now, bending over the trestle as far as he was able with his hands full of the weight of his calcified, imprisoned member, he exhibited in far more detail than I would commonly require the twin brown moons of his arse, skin stretched to his bending, and the puckered ring of his anus.

The trestle just too high and too narrow for him to rest the round weight upon, which weight required both his hands continuously, he was unable to use his hands to brace or steady himself. At the same time the freedom of his arms was impeded and as he bent, therefore, he teetered and groaned, the bulging weight that entrapped his cock and balls clearly dragging upon his groin.

Foolishly uncomprehending, briefly transfixed by the cyclopean gaze of the one brown eye peering up at me, I gazed first at his unwelcome and substantial fleshy display and then upon the instrument June was putting into my hand. I was startled. I might describe it simply as a cat-o-nine-tails, save that it had but five and each a braided hempen strap two thumb-widths broad.

Everything I'd been called upon to do up to this point had had to with love, with sex and with fertility. Why then did it now appear that I was expected to flay the arse of a slave whose cock was imprisoned in stone and who moved already bent and yet somehow still unbroken by its weight?

Chapter the Seventh

In which I deliver retribution
and discover new joys in gentle girls.

A shake of Summer's head catching my eye, she made the matter simpler with a no-less-simple mime, the moving of a finger, the simple simulation of the adjustment of a thong.

I had already observed that whilst men went about their business naked, save sometimes for paint and sundry forms of minor decoration, and exhibited their cocks with what seemed a natural, quiet pride, most females of pubescent and post pubic age wore a vestigial thong of coloured, braided twine. Concealing naught save perhaps the bud itself, I had wondered at its function, if indeed it had any function save decoration.

To those accustomed to draping themselves with manifold layers of cloth it is perhaps difficult to convey the effect of the near-ubiquity of this ephemeral nether-garment upon my own sense of profound nakedness. I had no thong, nor was I offered one, and my girls—uncommonly, it seemed, for their age—did not sport one either. Even in the first intimacy of sharing a meal together, seated upon the floor, more had been disclosed to me than I had ever imagined, in my prior life, that I would set eyes upon.

What meant it, then, this garment? Though I would not learn the entirety of it and all its subtleties until much later and my acquisition of sufficient language, curiosity drove me to attempt to find out what I could and had drawn me, again, to our tablet of sand.

I had drawn a simple body outline, indicating breasts and cunny, placing beside it with a simple loop and curve a drawing of a thong before superimposing the lines of the garment upon the figure itself. Ever astute, both girls seemed immediately to grasp the nature of my enquiry. Answering it was another matter, and not without either humour or drama.

Pointing at the drawn thong, I then pointed at June and sought to frame an expression of patent curiosity. Since neither immediately responded, I then did the same with Summer, who nodded and engaged June in brief conversation.

June it was who now placed the wooden cock between her thighs and moved to stand a pace or two distant from Summer. Summer first crouched down, making herself small, and placing her own thumb between her lips began to suck upon it, her expression sweetly child-like. June, meanwhile, repeatedly directed sidelong glances in the direction of her friend and saw, therefore, as I did, Summer raise her body by stages to the upright, relinquishing her thumb as, in effect, she 'grew up'.

How full my heart was as I gazed upon her, witnessing her discovery of adulthood as she toyed, her expression mystified, her eyes wide, with her breasts, as I saw the surprise in the eyes she lifted towards me as she fingered the soft down on her mound.

Seeing me nod, Summer looked toward June who, for her part, was carefully easing the formerly recumbent wooden cock up to and beyond the horizontal whilst fixing on Summer an almost comical expression of desire. It was at this point that Summer, affecting displeasure at the other's interest, mimed the act of dressing, of tying on the thong.

Modesty, then, at puberty. I could only nod and smile.

The girls, however, took the explanation further, Summer's disdainful expression changing in repeated glances at June to one of interest, culminating in a nod clearly of assent. As June moved towards her, holding out her arms to embrace her, Summer no less clearly mimed setting the thong aside before taking her lover in her arms.

A murmured exchange taking place between them, the two girls parted and resumed much their previous positions, Summer again disdainful, June clearly lusting. This time June's expression shifted, growing dark and cruel, and after a moment of brooding thus she strode purposefully forward, caught Summer by her hair and forced her legs apart with her own, inserting the wooden cock between their bodies.

Expression, posture, action and reaction were so startlingly redolent of violence that I was forced to check in myself an urge to intervene. Both girls, though, were looking at me, their eyes beseeching my attention, and I nodded, watching carefully.

June holding the wooden cock aside, Summer gently traced the outline of the imaginary thong, reminding me of its presence. When again I nodded, her fingers moved once more, tracing the outline of the under-cord anew. It passed no longer between those sweet lips. And lest I did not fully understand, both stepped up now to the sand-tray, Summer re-drawing the line, her face a grimace of anger and disgust.

I understood. So dark a cloud had these moments cast that a long embrace and a full night's sleep were scarce enough to dispel it.

Thus did I understand, from that slight gesture viewed across the twin mounds of the penitent's over-bent arse, the meaning of this day's events. Even now as this small woman stood gazing down at her diminutive feet I could see the sweet little buds between her legs which embraced the poignantly emblematic twine, and like her those lips were most petite. And yet this bastard had raped her.

The consequences for the girl, I could barely guess at, but for me a pall was cast, an unwonted stain impinging upon our own sweet Eden. Again I glanced at Summer, saw her anger a deeper, darker echo of my own, saw the swift stroke of her hand through silent air, and even as she completed that forceful gesture she held both her hands up, displaying very clearly her two thumbs and her eight fingers.

I was moved for the tiny creature who stood there still so downcast, seemingly as unwillingly bound to him as he was to her by the symbolic cord between them, which hung trailing from her hand whilst she looked neither at him nor at me, but gazed awkwardly and uncomfortably towards her tiny feet. And I was moved by the thought that she could have been mine. It could have been Summer standing there, or June—or me. And then it hit me that she was mine, one of mine, one of my children, my flock, my congregation.

I don't know if I truly meant to hit him as hard as then I did, the stroke sharp as a gunshot in our silent room as the five hempen tongues smote him across his cheeks, and as he yelped in pain and—it seemed—surprise, I saw Summer grinning with a hardness I'd not yet seen in her and June's eyes were brightly gleaming, her face a grimace of satisfaction.

And I must have meant it, for as Summer bent one little finger, and told me thus there were nine strokes left to go, my second strike at the roundly quivering flesh exploded the silent air again and this time the bastard screamed.

Two fingers down and I smote again on flesh where crimson bands were glowing, aiming for its puckered centre, and the man began to sob. Only now the girl was looking at me, a look of such mute gratitude upon her face as I had never known.

By the time Summer lowered her last little finger our subject was no longer bending—his knees had given way quite altogether and he hung suspended, rocking, crimson-arsed upon the trestle cross-bar, still clutching at the dreadful weight between his upper thighs which, loosed, would pull his groin apart. And Summer opened her hand again, her gaze directly into mine, and I knew she'd played me, kept the next ten strokes a secret to the very last moment.

I no longer needed to strike so hard, I had hurt him much already and sounds of anguish rose from the scourged offender continuously and unbroken. On my fourteenth stroke the girl who had brought him raised up her own hand in the simple gesture: 'Stop'. Summer nodding, I knew it must be her right.

Not a one of us moved to succour the man in any way but we simply waited till he was sufficiently recovered to raise himself from the punishment bar, lift the dragging weight on his member and shuffle towards the door. The girl drew sharply on the rope, reminding him who went first and bestowed on me a gentle smile that I shall always remember.

When she had passed beyond the curtain my Summer and my June approached me, placed their arms around me and embraced me. Much as I enjoyed it I was puzzled for the moment by this close attention and they sensed it. It was time for another simple mime and June, placing one of our stock of wooden cocks ball-end within her cleft held a sharpened quill across it, showed me she played Gorrogo, and took the 'cat of five tails' in her hand.

Summer meanwhile was bending gracefully over the trestle. Beneath the dimples aside her spine the ripe fruits of her arse swelled roundly, lusciously towards me, and already—despite myself—I felt a moistening, a hunger to reach out and to touch. But she was twisting, to look at me, and June-Gorrogo interceded, studying 'his' fingernails, glancing round, showing every sign of inattention, whilst carelessly, effortlessly flicking the hempen thongs against the other girl's unmarked and unmarking arse.

And I understood. Perhaps because he is a man, perhaps because the offender and he share some history, Gorrogo—who had the task before me—was too gentle in his punishment of the offender and, in that gentleness, undermined its very point and purpose. No wonder that look of disdain. No wonder the surprise in his first pained scream.

Our people, I will learn, believe in modest but effective retribution and retribution which is seen to be done. In this case the girl is lawfully entitled to beat him about the arse or elsewhere if she wants to, whenever she wants to, though she's not expected to kill or maim him, and if and when she wants to she can bring him to the appropriate officer of justice to undertake the task. Being able to inflict punishment on him for the wrong he did to her, and able to watch others inflict punishment on her behalf, is intended to sate her need for vengeance and make it clear that the sympathy of others lies with her, the victim.

At the same time, in this case, her violator is forced to become dependent upon her for almost everything. Another is appointed to relieve her when she wants it, especially of more noisome tasks, but it is up to her whether he is fed or not, whether he's allowed to lie down to sleep or not, or whether he's cleaned of his mess. Frequently she will actually spoon-feed him. Forced to follow closely round behind the lovely arse that did so tempt him and unable to do anything about it because what was previously his cock is now a useless burden to him, unable to reach her with his hands because they are needfully occupied keeping his cock and balls attached to him and unable, for associated reasons, to run away, he has to become her victim, to discover what it means to depend upon the kindness and charity of those offended against.

Though nothing had stirred within my nethers when I beat the prisoner, I was stirring even as I reflected upon my thoughts, upon the events and on the memory of Summer's lovely bending arse, her peeping brown eye, and the sight of June—however playfully—belaying her. It woke my hunger, somewhat, and that worried me.

There was one petitioner left, that day, but first a walk—our first for a time—and Summer and June and I strolled about the village naked, arm in arm, watching our villagers about their lives and work, watching the children play, the livestock peck and truffle in the ground.

And outside our door as we passed stood a table now, with that statuette of myself upon it that Arshon brought, and laden with provender and materials—an exquisitely engraved coconut cup (from the maker of the love-throne), piles of fruit, vegetables, fish, feathers, an exquisite animal fur (with the exquisite animal still in it, but I'll not go into that), a hand-carved comb, a sharks' tooth necklace, and more besides.

This is how I was kept and provided for. The villagers made offerings, the girls put them to our own use or traded them for other needful things, and everyone here considered adult had access to my cunny in return.

I noticed on my walk that the block in the centre of the compound was indeed a butcher's block, mainly—as it turned out— for feasts and festivals, and that the ever dutiful guards remained by my door and did not follow us. My hosts were welcoming, friendly and trusting, everyone glad to see me, offering grins and courteous bows which would not have seemed out place in London (in somewhat different attire, of course).

Mothers offered me their naked children to hold, as if doing so portended a safer future for the infants, older girls, pre-pubescent yet, looked up at me with wondering, doe-like eyes, peering from under impossibly long lashes, and boys approaching a similar age peered anxiously at me from behind their mothers, hiding behind where their mothers' skirts might have been.

The girls and I returned to the stream to bathe among its silken waters and I watched them play, enjoyed the shade, and felt glad to be alive.

Home again, and we encountered our final supplicant of the day. Another woman, this time desiring that the vastly evident swelling in her belly might arrive as a boy-child to please her husband, and not prove yet another filly—or so in mime and picture Summer and June subsequently explained it. The pregnancy already so far advanced it struck me as deeply poignant and touching that she believed she could draw from me something which would add a pizzle if it were not already there, but for the moment I was aware of her most as yet another demand on my cunny.

They would all have their reasons, and my girls would be able to explain many of them, but they did not know in advance who would arrive at our door, and their hesitant mimes and drawings frequently occurred after the blessing, in whatever form, was given. In time of course I would know all the reasons, for the gift of a blessing needed sanctioning, unless I freely volunteered it. It could be gifted, ironically, by the king, one man who's steaming yard and juice I'd have been only too glad to accommodate and could not, and who held in his hands—as it were—the very fate, the life and death, of my poor pink slit. Otherwise the gift required to be reasoned for, and it was June and Summer who decided the yea or nay, who heard and tried the case and sentenced me or not. I would find they rarely disallowed, were generous to a fault with my appendages, but neither were they, when called upon, noticeably ungenerous with their own.

I resigned myself, thus, to my seat upon the love-throne, placed my vulnerable pendant parts within the aperture of the target and watched as the solicitous girls gently coaxed the oddly fragile largeness of her onto the bench and backrest, manoeuvred her into position.

I could feel her breath cool against the heat that is already there, feel my lips emboldening, my nipples drawing the skin more taut upon the flesh of my bosoms, and she touched me.

Perhaps there was unwonted desperation in her desire for a son, perhaps it was that her belly's engorgement had over-long prevented, physically or attitudinally, fulfilling sexual congress with the baby's father, but, for whatever cause, she now attacked me with a voluptuous passion of lip and tongue surpassing aught that I had known, the pearl of my clit seeming to leap with eager alacrity from the protection of its swelling pink surrounding nacre, desperate for what that moist tongue offered.

As always then my thoughts were flitting from one encounter to the next and in my head I caught flashes almost of them all—of the big woman bouncing on her husband's cock, the contorted face of the arrogant warrior as I milked his fine engorgement, of Arshon leaning forward in blindness of passion to kiss his queen through my very own lips, felt upon and within my very own cunny, and the two raised arses, the criminal's seared and crimsoned with stripes of passionate agony, my Summer's so sweet, so sweetly curvaceous, and clean.

I tried to focus elsewhere, but everything I saw—the room, our golden drape, the girls, the board with its collected sexual ephemera, recalled it all, and even looking down upon that heaving body beneath me, the glorious dark brown burgeoning circumference of fecundity, even darker and oilier in its film of sweat, skin stretched taut as a drum by the surging life within it, drove me deeper into need.

A massive heat was building within me, my vulva volcanic and erupting, seething waves of heat surging to my nipples, my neck, my lips, breaking beads of perspiration on my brow,

moistening my hair with sweat. My flushed arse cheeks pushed
hard down on the seating timber, my groin seeking to drag me
through the enclosing wood, forced more of me into that warm,
wet, luscious, lusting maw.

She was as one gifted by the gods and her tongue was lithe
and firm and soft and mobile, tickling, stroking, dipping, drawing, ever moistening; knowing somehow when *she* was numb
and resting her, playing round her till she woke, driving and
driving me to the gush, almost—but no, not—beyond.

My waters prematurely breaking, my child beneath me came
away, weeping joy and gratitude, yet leaving me yearning, wanting and hungry as my midwives walked her to the door.

The day was darkening, torches flared beyond the curtain,
and I was weary, and, moreover, at least a little sore.

Food, next, and for me a brandy which, mingling with the
earlier whiskey, softened me, warmed me, and June and Summer laid me down and bathed me, exquisitely gently, especially
of *her*, who is hurting, and whom both of them examine closely,
deftly, with sweet concern. And then an oiling and hands moving
and pulling and softening, and an unguent then upon her which
chills and chills and I needed to make water. With this, too, they
helped me, and afterwards cleansed her, and gentling me softly
again moistly touch her, the chill of the lotion like ice on my clit
and no waters to trigger.

The hurt gently easing I sat in our bed watching them sharing their evening bathing, and listening to their soft sweet brown
voices, hearing them chuckle and giggle and laugh, soft-wishing
I knew why and that I might share it more nearly.

So vividly still do I recall that to mind. The blessed sponge
slides in the soft hand of Summer, sweeps sweet curves of shoulder ere gliding smooth down, tracing the back to the backside
of June, and dips down beneath her, or rises and rolls in June's
plump little grasp and kneads the ripe bubbies of Summer, wor-
ships the curve of her belly, sweeps into the vee of her valley.

Were I but that sponge, dear Heaven, I yearned, were I but that
sponge! I was the goddess, yet it was I who was the worshipper,

whose heart ached with longing and love. I truly adored them, in their wondrous completeness, that heart-breaking wholeness of each.

Our house was abundant of manifold treasures and all of them mine, yet I knew full well that nought needed accounting, and everything sat in its place. Everything that must be done I saw them do, sometimes turn by turn without discussion, but at other times one would turn her hand to a particular task, even a noisome one, repeatedly. They bickered not about who did this or that, just did, and all of it smiling, eyes and mouths together. And their attention to me was as to a worshipped child—ever gentle, all forgiving, sometimes gently persistent if I were stubborn, yet never forcing, never angry.

And it struck me as I watched them that as they felt for me so I felt for them, the same sense of joy at every new discovery about them, at every new sound, new scent, a deep, calm, trusting adoration.

I watched Summer light the oil lamp in the corner, June check the curtain at the door, then both were padding softly towards me, their skins dully glowing, then nestling down beside me on the floor. Still too warm for covers yet, they lay with me between them, and June's hand moving slow around my thigh, descended and touched me gently. Prepared to flinch, I did not, for what pain there was was gone, and she, now sitting up, gently oiled me, made me warm with slippery fingers whilst Summer, turned towards me, stroked my hair.

Now both of them beside me, on their elbows, two shadowy faces looking gently into mine, lamp-light delineating curve of nose and cheek and chin, golden catch-lights in their eyes and sleek black hair, and smiles in shadow, I heard the lovely words, so gentle:

"Sum-mah, Joo-Oon, fucking Me Lady?"

I answered softly, "Oh yes!"

Were fucking only always so, thus gentle and thus kind.

Wearing nought but a softly conspiratorial smile betwixt them they had turned and partly over-lay me, my right breast pressed beneath Summer, my left beneath June, and whilst both girls trawled gentle fingers through my garden, June leaned in to kiss me. Softly first, our lips warm cushions between us, then her tongue began gently questing, prising my lips open till our teeth touched, tongues caressed.

She was sweet as sugar within, so soft and moist, and eager from their first soft words I felt my valley flooding with the heat of wanting, keening with the need of them because she was yet untouched.

June's lips held fast with their moist, warm, soft adhesion, her nose caressing mine as she breathed my breath, as I breathed hers, feeling her belly tumescent as I exhaled, feeling mine swell with her breath in me. Consuming the air which passes soft between us I felt my mind begin to float and suddenly she was gone, air rushing into my craving mouth and nostrils, and the same moist lips softly gripped around my teat.

June having parted from me, smiling Summer lays her gentle lips on mine and I'm feeling them, and then her tongue, and then I am breathing her, tasting the subtly different tastes within the mouth of her, my left breast aching to June's silken tongue caressing, my groin aflame with still unrequited wanting, and then I can breathe again and Summer takes my other breast, both girls suckling and kneading just like babes.

But their hands act not as babies' hands but stroke and explore, soft fingers and palms caressing and sliding, up, over, down, under, along and every which way, sometimes scoring gently with their nails, and I am arching in the blindness of my feeling, four hands caressing without pattern, keeping me wanting, keeping me wondering.

June slides upon my chest, cunny sweet upon my belly, playing with my hot, hard teats and kneading at my softness, whilst Summer, this time, slips softly down beneath me, her tongue wet first so close to where June presses on me that I know she must have wet her too, then slithering warm, sending cold sharp shivers down inside me, her tongue draws a moist path down along me, drawing nearer, ever nearer.

She is there. My groin dry hot in an agony of wanting, bucks as her tongue touches coldly on my clit, and my hands grasping and trembling with wanting are suddenly full of little June's bubbies, so sweetly soft, their peaks so poignantly hard, and I knead them, and she's smiling, understanding my wanting.

Understanding my wanting. Pressing on the knees bestriding me, raising the soft pressure of her little cunny from me, June lifts herself and a hand of hers takes mine and places it, so gently, there, and holds it, so gently, there, and I feel my fingers moving, dancing to their tune of longing, sliding now within her and pressing on the bone.

I have never touched deep in another woman's wetness, and even as I do so, Summer does the same to mine, and as I feel her fingers sliding and probing I seek to follow their rhythm in the girl poised, arched, above me, pressing herself up now from the hands small and firm upon my breasts. My fingers long and slender, even more than Summer's own, are reaching and touching as they never have before, worshipping within the moist, unseen cathedral of my June, feeling strange, and new, and holy.

My breasts hot and bullet-peaked beneath my darling's hands, surging heat within my loins makes me twist and writhe with wanting whilst above me little June begins the same. My nether lips in sweet engorgement tingle and burn inside the warm-wet mouth of Summer, her soft tongue trysting gently with my peeping pearl, sliding liquid deep inside my cunny, and I'm conscious of a hunger I have never known before.

My hands are full of June's round arse cheeks, know their silk-soft firmness, and grasping firmly pull her forward, and she knows.

She does not hesitate. I have not overstepped the line.

The soft, sweat-wet rivulet of down on the mound of her softly kissing my nose, I inhale her wondrous woman scent, open my mouth and engulf her, feeling the heat of her thighs about my face. The faintest hint of something that is acrid in her scent, no little touch somehow of coconut and lime, the first taste of that wondrous orifice contains them all, and almond and human salt in wondrous wetness.

Here by touch of tongue alone I find the small, hard, silken bud that is her glorious nestling pearl and touch it, caress it, seeking to adore it with my tongue. This is worship. I am at the very core of her, that tiny privy place, admitted to the temple of the woman, and I seek now to speak to it in tongues, dipping and flicking and lapping 'I love you, I love you' over and over and over again, and I hear her mewing.

And hot and wet of face with her fluids and with mine and hot and wet of cunny with fluids both of mine and of Summer, I feel the sweet proboscis slide, that simulate of manhood venturing softer into me than ever a man has done, questing soft and probing, now driving, delving harder, firmer, driving and driving me.

I might not have so congratulated myself upon my own artistry with the young warrior had I but begun to recognise the artistry that was theirs, for as if in jest at what I had done to him Summer now did the same to me, driving me onward and upward to that precious brink ere letting me slide before I can fall, and driven by a want become a need become an aching craving now knotted beneath my belly, flashing lightning throughout my womanhood and searing at my breast, I drive my tongue with greater and yet greater passion, lapping and diving, soaring within her till my June squeals a muted squeal, arches backward and sideways, falls softly from me.

Rigid, now, with craving, I feel heart-break in her going, a ravening hunger for more, and Summer, bedamned, is easing again.

A fresh thrust, suddenly, a tongue too upon my aching, wanting bud, and miraculously I was full again with the wondrous taste and texture of woman. Only it was different. No sweeter, no better, only different. For it was Summer.

I mutter cunny-muffled words, 'I love you, I love you' through a mouth that is full of her soft, woman's sweetness, stroking the lips of her, tongue teasing them open, questing and seeking and freshly alighting on glorious firmness of pearl.

Bodies rising and falling with surges of needing she is riding my face like a wave and I love her, drawing her deep in my mouth I would swallow her whole if I could, feeding a hunger I have never known, and June's tongue caressing and the big cock now plunging, I am sweeping upward again.

The tide of Summer's wave breaks with her coming, flows over me foaming, stunning my senses with her taste and her crying, and I'm gone and I'm flying and gushing and falling and I would be screaming if she did not fill me still.

And, after, I'm shaking, and all of us holding, all of us one in our wet scents and feeling, each of us weeping and smiling with joy and each of us loving.

From that evening, it seems to me, did my life truly begin, and so—though I could not then know it—was it destined to continue for some time. In the consensual giving of my two angels, their wonderful solicitousness of me which somehow bred in me the same deep care for them, I had found—despite the demands that would follow—a joy such as I had never known.

It did seem, too, beyond reason at times that such an idyllic place could exist unspoiled, and it would be easy to assume that my vision of it is coloured by the pleasure of my memory, that there were evils and dangers I have chosen to forget.

In truth there were evils, but few. There were those among the tribe who fought and argued amongst themselves, just as among any tribe of our own; and tropic isles—except in foolish fantasies—are not without their dangers. Insects, poisonous reptiles, even places of danger, tantalising berries which can make most efficacious medicine but which, to one unknowing, may prove deadly.

My life among my people—the happiest time I had ever known—was not to be without its dangerous experiences or its potential embarrassments.

Chapter the Eighth

*In which I find quite unexpected delight in matrimony
and meet a thorough pig.*

I f passing waste had once seemed to me to render doubt-
ful the godliness of my nature, there was one other matter
which, in logic, should have posed a greater threat, and yet
I swear I'd given it not a thought until the day late in my second
week when Summer disappeared, going out alone one afternoon
and simply not returning.

I could easily have been beside myself, had June not been so
smilingly solicitous and careful in encouraging me, in such ways
as she could discover, that Summer would soon return.

Unable to make a convincing drawing that I might easily understand the matter, June went to our pile of powders and medi-
caments, chose a dark red earthy substance and, mixing it with
but a little water, produced a remarkable semblance of blood. I
was immediately and nonsensically affrighted, too easily imagining Summer lying wounded, far from me, being kept from me
and dying. Only then June dripped a very few drops within the
cleft of her cunny.

The curse! Ye Gods! The curse! And mine must surely follow,
as certain as day follows night, and I'd given it not a thought!
They'll not be queuing for cunnilingus then, methinks! And I am
undone, for what of all things could prove me the more human?

It did not, of course, turn out thus.

Convinced I understood the cause, June led me from the
house and upon a walk, passing a few words with the supervis-
ing guards equivalent—I must suppose—with posting the notice
'gone fishing'. Indeed we went toward the stream, but then, passing through it, followed a clearly-delineated but well-hidden trail
up the side of the hill. Coming at one point to a fork I met my predecessor—not Gorrogo, but a statue crudely carved of soft stone
and femininely accoutred with improbably wide hips, vast—if

somewhat pockmarked—bubbies and a deeply-graven, large slit with a hole at its base. Over many years the hole in the stone cunny had begun to show serious signs of wear and, frankly, I knew how she felt.

On this occasion we took the fork in the path to the right, leaving me fleetingly curious as to what might lie to the left, and proceeded deep into forest, surrounded by the sounds of birds and insects, passing quietly as a dream through the green-tinted twilight of the forest's mystery. A little time brought us to a small house much like our own except that it stood within a tall, encircling wall which, being vastly overgrown, hid the dwelling place almost completely.

Here, with only a tame parrot for company, we found Summer, and great was the hugging that followed, though I discovered she was far from unhappy where she was and no doubt counted it a useful opportunity to escape from our business, to rest and contemplate.

Here in seclusion she would remain until her bleeding time was past, June assisting me at my work, and when June 'fell' it would fall to Summer to take up her part of the duties until June could return. I would learn that the village possessed its own menstruation house, not far from the settlement and which the ladies of the village were inclined to treat rather as a holiday home. The special nature of my servitors did not permit them to share it, and required them to have this place of their own which was kept a closely-guarded secret. When my turn came—and when it did they evidenced no surprise—I became sequestered also, only unlike them, initially, I had them both for company, the acolytes being apparently superfluous in the absence of their goddess.

In the shortest time, of course, that miracle occurred which causes women who live together to share even that special cycle, so that our absences became anyway contiguous, and we came to much enjoy these times together, being quiet and close, having the time to think and learn. Betwixt us we transformed the little house into quite a happy den, surreptitiously transferring many other of my possessions to it.

I must turn, now, my hoped-for reader, to a matter of some significance perhaps, because, to my recollection, the memoirs of other castaways seem rather to demand it. I had grown remiss, I must admit, about the matter of time. Coming from a world of diaries and appointments, of fashionable time-pieces and fashionable time-keeping, I am sure the matter should have preoccupied me more than it did, but I did not permit it. Partly this was because I was not entirely certain of the date when the Talisman struck, partly because I was uncertain as to how long I'd remained unconscious in Smythe's boat and largely because I rather didn't care. No great, carved post for me, then, notched with the days and the phases of the moon, no etchings into cave walls, nor scrapings in the sand in order to allow me to know with certainty when Tuesday gave way to Wednesday or when the century turned.

Unlike other, more famous castaways, of whom, like myself, you may have read, the island never seemed to me a place of incarceration. Indeed I felt quickly liberated by what had happened to me and never learned to count the hours and days in the manner only prisoners, castaways and children awaiting Christmas appear to do. Nor indeed, and this matter is related, did I keep tireless watch—or, indeed, any watch—for a 'civilised' ship which might effect my 'rescue'. England and all I had known seemed millions, rather than paltry thousands, of miles away.

My islanders kept their own calendar, determined by seasons and phases of the moon observed more acutely than I was capable of doing, and since their calendar rather determined my life I was happy to live in accordance with it. In consequence it is difficult for me to be very specific about the dates of subsequent events.

Within my first few days upon the island, you will recall, I had blessed—besides my rather large reception committee—two couples seeking babies, a small man seeking an erection, a carpenter, two graduating warriors, a pregnant mother desirous of a boy child and, I suppose, Gorrogo himself, and delivered punishment for the first time to a rapist.

In ensuing weeks and months I would find these duties rep-
licated, sometimes with small variations, and in due course I
would learn other duties. Some few of these would come over
time to be routine, some annual or seasonal in the manner of Easter, Christmas or Harvest Thanksgiving. And some would have
it in common with Easter and Christmas at home in being regularly occurring, often requiring more of us than we might care
to contribute, and involving us more closely sometimes than we
wish with people we don't overmuch care for.

I was their Aphrodite, their goddess of love, and aught that
had anything to do with love and fecundity they brought to me.
Some tasks were more arduous than others, whilst others repeatedly revealed—it seemed to me—the miraculous nature of our
people.

Hardest of the tasks allotted to me, given that I had no faith
in my own capacity to assist with anything, was that of blessing
a barren woman. Fortunately barrenness would prove rare, but
never did I feel more fraudulent, nor—given what was expected
of me—could I have been more grateful for what I had learned
and experienced through June and Summer.

Whilst I had remained seated in my love throne they helped
lay the woman prostrate on the bench, and when I descended
they explained to me in whispers and in some of the few words
of their language I had learned: "She no babies make". Summer
then placed a rather large cock-toy in my hand and whispered in
my ear quite happily; "Must first make she wet with tongue".

My disciples' role, I discovered, was to suspend my supplicant's legs in the air, knees bent, to allow me freer access, and
delivering cunnilingus to another, even if she was a stranger, was
at least a change and a respite for my own pink cleft. I did have
qualms, in truth, for I have seen and heard enough to know that
the hunger for a child of one's own is the keenest and most deso-
late hunger perhaps that any woman may know.

It irked me, too, that the husband was not present on either
of the two occasions on which I performed this duty, for I sensed,
and subsequently learned, that that fact demonstrated my peo-

ple's belief that barrenness was a condition of the woman alone, a singular inequality given their beliefs in most other matters.

Just twice, then, was I to perform this, for the women concerned did not return for second visits, and the rather spectacular inner explosions, joyous cries and screams my ministrations happily produced seemed to me a very poor consolation at the time. I can at least report, though, that one of the women did go on to have a child of her own (in fact by availing herself of another man) and though I had to wait some time to achieve a full understanding of what she meant, Summer was able to set me more at ease regarding the fate of the second.

Whilst our people considered barrenness a misfortune, they did not, at least, consider it demeaning or belittling. Once a given term had passed, following my ministration, and no infant was produced, the will of the goddess was accepted and the woman concerned busied herself, as did most of the village women, with everybody else's children. Family, here, had a far broader meaning than ever I had known it to have in England.

Most delightful of the ceremonies I was called on to perform must, I think, be that of marriage.

Quite what the purpose of marriage was, given the gentle laxity of our people's requirements regarding sexual behaviour, I was never to be quite sure, though over time I rather came to believe that it was both a sweet celebration of that which we call love—the deep spiritual and physical desire for one particular other—and a delightful excuse for dancing and merriment.

Betrothals occurred with great spontaneity, there being almost no exchanges of property involved among people who owned so little and shared what little they had, and requiring not much more than the consent and desire of the couples who became betrothed. And since the pair concerned had probably been rutting for some time with the single-minded determination of rabbits, the formal period of courtship only really lasted from the moment of betrothal to the instant the celebration could be practically arranged, frequently a matter of hours and rarely more than days.

A few weeks after my arrival, then, I was introduced to two young people who walked into the house arm in arm and bathing in such a mutual glow of adoration that their purpose required very little explanation. Summer having coaxed me down from the love throne as the two youngsters knelt then guided me gently into position, first before him and then before her, that they might take their blessings just as had the warriors I first met on the beach.

Since both were fairly assiduous in partaking of that blessing and produced both an urgent trembling in my loins and a shivering weakness in my knees, I had rather assumed that that would be the end of it. Rather delightfully, it was not.

When the wedding feast began, around noon some two days later, I found myself, not unusually, being bathed and dried by both my girls. Interpreting their looks and gestures I then remained standing, and was rather astonished when they returned to me and began to rub a white, oily substance into my skin. Adhering as it dried, and really quite uncomfortable, I was rendered white as a ghost, my natural pinkness visible—as my vanity mirror disclosed—in an unpainted diamond at the base of my back and in the area, also left unpainted, of my vulva.

Still beaming at me, Summer then placed a headdress of tall white feathers upon my golden hair and gestured me to stand upon the love throne's bench, whereupon four warriors, also painted rather ghastly white entered the house and raised me on a chair of arms, much as their contemporaries had done that first day on the beach.

Thus was I borne aloft to the centre of the village, followed by my two girls, and deposited on a platform which had been raised there. Guided by my girls, again, I stood there, naked but for my coat of paint and my feather headdress, under the cheerful gaze of the larger part of the community.

It was most fortunate that the lapse of time, brief as it was, between the betrothal and the marriage had been sufficient for June and Summer to demonstrate—still in mime and drawings in those days—just what it was I was required to do. And my head filled to bursting with the images with which they had presented me, my loins, I must admit, were churning in a most disturbing manner.

Compelled to remain standing thus, naked before the eyes of all, for the duration of the wedding speeches, made at no brief length by Arshon, the couple's fathers and sundry other long-winded individuals, my knees grew rather tired even before the girl was brought to me, lifted kneeling onto the dais. Shuffling on her knees towards me until she felt my hands alight upon her shoulders, she paused only for so long as it took me to bend and kiss her, as I had my first ever supplicants on the island, upon the crown of the head, ere she began to assault me with her tongue.

In the strangeness of the situation and anticipating what I understood was to follow—hoping that I had understood it correctly—I was already inflamed, my cunny burning, my body shivering and rippling within like the surface of a mill-pond in high wind. And this time her task—her given task—was to please me, to satisfy the goddess with her tongue, rather than merely to obtain a blessing for herself.

I was presented with a most unusual difficulty. The purpose of her ministering to me was to demonstrate her capacity as a lover, and lest I was to undermine her marriage from the very start it remained to me to amply prove my satisfaction. The means, however, and the only means for one who was compelled to remain standing throughout, was not one that came easily—not with so large and expectant an audience.

I had no choice, however, and, in truth, the glorious mechanism of her tongue did make the matter easier. I screamed.

Standing on a raised platform, surrounded by some two hundred people, I extended my arms as if her tongue was the nail of my crucifixion, tilted my head to the sky and screamed a long and ululating scream which brought the audience to its feet, shouting and stamping and clapping applause.

Only when I could bring my hands back to her shoulders, and my skills for such navigation were sorely undermined, did the girl desist. Had my own girls not come to my aid, supporting me beneath my arms, I doubt I would have managed to deliver the final head kiss which brought that part of the proceedings to an end. But it was his turn now, and I was joyful.

He had been well coached, I saw, and delivered like the girl on his knees he but kissed my quim as I performed the initial head kiss and then, as I stepped back, he lowered himself to the floor of the dais, rolled over onto his back.

Trying not to stare at the vast erection already being applauded by our audience I truly felt my mouth begin to water, but it was not my mouth, for once, that would be blessed or blessing.

My girls knelt down beside him, played him for the congregation's greater amusement, first taking turns at sucking him for some moments before sliding onto his cock the sheath-skin Gorrogo had delivered and carefully tying its cord around his swollen balls. Ere that was finished the fullness of his flushed and vein-knotted member was truly prodigious indeed.

Scarcely able to believe my fortune, struggling to conceal a grin of sheer delight, I stepped over and above him, facing towards his feet, lowered myself toward him and slid my flushed pink opening, still wet from his own bride's tongue, slowly down upon his fullness. Oh joy, my reader, to be thus full again, and oh how I wished, that moment, that I could suspend time itself!

The requirement of my elevation had not done the poor boy any favour, yet his upward thrusts were anything but feeble and provided a joyous reminder of what it was to be fucked, and properly, by a lusting man. My girls' own ministrations, the presence of the audience and his own real need to prove to the watching world his prowess, might well have been too much for him. I was quite prepared to feel his shrinking to insignificance within my clenching, hungry shaft and to pretend, if need be, to a satisfaction that would ever afterwards perplex him, but it did not happen.

That Summer and June were both helping hold me in position and at the same time using one free hand each to stroke and pet him may well have assisted, but he preserved throughout that concentrated focus on pleasuring my cunny that all men should be forced to learn, and gave me no little joy.

Even through his sheath I felt him, so hard was I clenched about him, my hungry flesh and muscle clutching at such unwonted satisfaction with the desperation of a drowning man to a piece of driftwood. And long before I felt him come, I began to loose every atom of sensation in me, shaping the tremors and lightning flashes already exploding from my loins into sound, gasping vocally, moaning loudly, weaving my body in a drunken swaying dance around his prong in a manner which both impressed my audience and, I found, contributed no little additional pleasure to my cunny.

Our happy observers were already applauding when I heard quite distinctly his own tortured, gurgling cry of release and felt him surge, just as she did, and no triumph of the London stage has ever been better received than the sperm-filled sheath so lovingly removed from him and held aloft in triumph. Had I been required to drink it down I could have, in the sheer effulgence of my joy, but it was kept for other purposes.

'Twas with the greatest difficulty, afterwards, and only with my lovely girls' support, that I could remain seated on the platform, drink and dine of my portion of the feast. I have little recollection of the evening that ensued, knowing only that I slept that night more deeply than I had in a very long time.

In the years that followed, marriages were to remain an occasion of particular joy to me, and were, in another form, to provide me with perhaps the greatest astonishment I had known.

On the first of several occasions I was again presented with a couple, equally arm in arm and equally glowing with mutual adoration, and learned that I was to prove their sexual suitability, be the vessel of their marriage I had been before. Only on these occasions the marrying couples were girls. That that between women which English law and custom would have persecuted and punished violently was so easily accepted here should not, of course, have surprised me, and the public cunnilingus with which they proved themselves on me was, I must admit, a source of most profound delight.

More amazing yet, to me, was the occasion I discovered a couple to be both men, though their proving promised to be more problematic. Whether such male bonding was rarer, or whether it simply proceeded without recourse to ceremony I do not know, but this was the only such marriage I was ever to witness, and it is fortunate for them, and was most fortunate for me, that both were somehow able to prove themselves within me and fill the sheath. Nor was the celebration of their doing so in any way diminished.

Nor were weddings the only feasts to which I would be delivered, my body painted, and to one of these, since it was significant in other respects and to the awakening of my slumbering sense of danger, we shall come later.

Within the first quarter year or so, learning to perform and putting into practice the duties I have disclosed, including my first marriage, the thought that danger might lurk on or about the island seemed never, really, to have impinged upon my consciousness. Never had I been happier, never had I felt more safe. The people, my people, never ceased to amaze and delight me.

There was almost no theft here, none claiming possession of much and all usually quite willing to share everything from the food on the table (as it were, for tables were actually scarce) to the marriage partner who lay in their bed. Their government comprised the king, who was expected to a marry a queen who would offer him wise counsel and who was permitted more than one queen should one of them prove pretty but vacuous, and though he was born the king it took but a vote of the populace to remove him and transfer the line of royal inheritance elsewhere. Thus the king must always be a diplomat, wary of his people's requirements.

The attitude of our people toward sex was, as I have already indicated, far beyond common English comprehension. In England a young woman spends hours at her toilette in endeavours to 'make herself beautiful' and will tell you she feels empowered when she has achieved this. Yet let the wrong man—or woman, for that matter—pass comment on how beautiful she is, or acknowledge it with a certain look or smile, and she's offended. Duels are fought, men are killed — and lovely cocks entirely wasted — in pursuit of this foolish game.

On the island there is but little that the village women can do, so much has nature blessed them, to beautify themselves. But that little they do anyway, adding dark colour around their eyes, reddening their lips and cheeks sometimes, drawing the thong a little tighter that it makes their lower lips the more pronounced, yet having done all or none of these things there is not a one who is not open to any compliment from any source.

During social events such as feasts and weddings, imbibing much of a sweet soft ale of their own brewing, behaviour becomes very flirtatious, and accompanied by the magnificently carnal dancing of some of the villagers, the situation can be much arousing. To discover she has engendered an erection in an attentive male is, to the woman, not a threat but a compliment, to be greeted with a smile, perhaps by some petting, and if she's so minded, by more. And this remains true even if she's wed, for convention requires of either husband or wife that they must only request their partner's permission first, before fucking their admirer of the moment. Permission is not easily withheld, since to withhold it suggests an ownership of the other which is not allowed, and congress between marrieds and lovers need never, therefore, be kept darkly and dangerously secret.

Which is not to say a native woman tups every male in whom she produces a hard-one, nor that they are in their nature hugely promiscuous, only that she always has the choice and signifies it, ultimately, by taking off — or not — her thong.

A paradise, then, for one such as I, long tired of the conventions that had bound me, kept me from my Sam, forced upon me the slender and unwilling penis of my distant husband. A fool's paradise? How safe, really, was I here?

I would have been safer, had I behaved more sanely!

The affair of the pig took place some three months or so after my arrival, for I kept, as I have said, no strict accounting — and almost ended my island sojourn.

Our people eat from a great many sources and most of these are small—fish, fruit, naturally occurring vegetables, nuts and coconuts, small animals, birds and the like—but for a feast or special occasion their meat of first choice is wild pig. Quite where these came from no-one seems to know, but there are tribes of these creatures upon the island and none here can remember a time when there were not. These pigs, then, are and were then sometimes hunted for meat, a process which is not without excitement since a furious boar can be really most dangerous.

Though I knew it not at the time, but had guessed something of the sort from the activity about our village, we were about to celebrate an annual festival. Part of what was celebrated was that a full moon was due, and this was always of itself an important event.

In consequence of the projected feast a number of parties were dispatched to hunt for wild boar, as they had done many times before, using—I would discover—a process similar to that employed on English shoots in that beaters drove the animals towards the weapons of the hunting party.

One such party found their prey almost on the outskirts of the village—something quite unheard of, the animals being so shy and reclusive—and the beaters jumping swiftly to the conclusion that this was some special provenance of Heaven launched their attack without properly scouting out the situation. In doing so, and breaking their own firm rule, they placed themselves in the gravest danger, for among the herd were suckling young, parents mad to protect them and a porcine elder statesman and warrior of quite legendary proportion.

In consequence the beaters found themselves under sudden and very dangerous attack before the hunters were close enough to act; a girl was badly mauled, and the others fled, straight for the village.

The one great boar pursued them all the way, and in his rage he must have been many times briefly deflected from his course, for otherwise he would have had, and hurt, many more of our people than he did.

The first I knew of this present danger was a deal of commotion outside the house and, rushing toward the doorway, I spied the creature standing in the middle of the common, snorting in a most bellicose fashion and stamping and tearing at the ground. That he was not stamping and tearing at anything more vulnerable is accounted for by the fact that every human being in the village had withdrawn within his or her own home, watching with frightened eyes from the darkness. Even my guards had withdrawn as far as they possibly could, clearly terrified of the furious, rampaging animal—and it's not to be wondered at.

The creature was huge, black, flaming-eyed, foaming-mouthed and equipped with a pair of tusks half the length of a grown man's arm, and possessed of a most aggressive demeanour—rather like a drunken rake who fancies he's been robbed by the whore for whom he can't get his cock up.

Forewarned of snakes and other creatures sometimes finding their way into homes I had made it my practice to keep Alfred's pistols—the workman-like affair with which I had shot him and the spectacular pair from the trunk—well-primed. I kept them un-cocked to prevent accidental discharge, and carefully wrapped in oil-cloth for protection, so they needed no more than unwrapping, cocking and simple priming to bring them quickly into action. Thus, now, I quickly prepared them.

I was terrified, frankly, but I could see that this creature was a real danger, not only to me but to those I loved, and not knowing how his presence had come about I had no idea that armed and skilful warriors were not very far behind him. I knew only that he must be dealt with and took upon myself the task.

Girding an old leather belt of Alfred's round me I slid one of the duelling pistols twixt it and my waist and flinched at its chill, cold hardness. A gun in each hand I then advanced, slowly and carefully, toward the posturing beast.

Not perhaps seeing me straight away, he stood his ground rather like some black knight of yore awaiting a challenger on the field of tourney, a picture of determined aggression, slowly moving his head from side to side for sight of an enemy. Some sound, perhaps, of my movement reaching his upright and twitching ears and alerting him to my presence, brought him round to face me as I moved slowly forward. His red eyes fixing upon me evilly, I was so sore afraid I thought the piss would fountain out of me at any moment, but he did nothing yet save stand and stare.

I continued drawing slowly nearer, not having held a pistol in years and knowing, anyway, how fickle they are, then—certain he was about to charge me, for he had lowered his head and was cleaving the ground with a fore-hoof—I raised the late Arthur's gun and fired.

I heard the click of the hammer, the scratch of the flint on steel, only to find myself staring stupefied at a resolutely un-discharged weapon. I dropped it to the ground only as the great boar chose to charge, and hearing a shrill scream I wondered if it was my own.

It seemed as if the whole world, all of nature, held its breath, as I gazed upon this charging, furious beast that seemed almost to flow, as if time were somehow suspended, a visible blur hanging in space. And of how what happened next happened, I have frankly not the slightest recollection, remembering only an explosion cataclysmic as the end of the world itself in the sweatingly pregnant, dreadful silence and standing half-blinded by smoke, waiting a dreadful long instant of silence for the searing agony of boar tusks ripping into me.

Instead I heard a shrill squealing. Discharging the duelling pistol from my left hand—not the hand I would ever have chosen to use—I had still hit the beast and had hurt it, the ball smashing into its fore-leg-shoulder and the impact throwing it over. Fallen awkwardly the beast now sought to rise, still with the use of three good legs, and with scarce a thought but to end it I stepped up far too close, drawing the pistol from my belt as I moved, and discharged the second shot between its eyes, ending its pain forever.

Such an event, of course, could scarcely be without consequences.

Chapter the Ninth

In which I am a heroine and sup the milk of human kindness.

W hen I had taken action against the pig—I shall not say 'when I decided to' since, to my chagrin, I do not believe any conscious consideration took place in my mind—no thought of import had impinged upon me save that those I loved were in danger. Somehow, therefore, it never struck me that I was embarking on a most significant and portentous endeavour, and an endeavour for which, in this culture, only men were trained.

Nor did I ever picture myself as others there would see me; stark naked but for a leathern belt, blonde, long-legged and nubile, gold hair blowing in the breeze, my own skin golden now (thank heaven I browned and did not burn as so many fair women do!). Add to this vision an alien weapon in each hand and another nosing into my golden muff, myself, their goddess incarnate, advancing toward a fearful monster and—without sign of fear that they could see—swiftly and fiercely disposing of it.

For the villagers it was the stuff of legend and enacted upon the special day when the new full moon, the very arse of their goddess, would hang brightly in the sky.

I did not know then, either, that the beast was one of great repute, was called the 'Black Devil' because of his propensity to harm, and had actually killed two people. It was primarily out of fear of this one infamous beast that they normally conducted their hunts with such cautious circumspection.

And so a tale was that day added to the tales they told around the fire, and I was to be worshipped as its heroine. As soon as this occurred to me I elected not to speculate upon what form that worship would take.

The festival itself, my first of these usually annual events, was novel to me, and a most exciting occasion. Beneath a violet velvet

sky the darkness of the earth and the structures around the compound were silver-gilt with shining moon-glow and splashed
with the flickering, dancing golden light of feasting fires and
torches. As usual the night was balmy, the kind of night when
European interlopers into paradises everywhere fretted in their
stays and corsets, plucked at wet and clinging clothing as it crept
coarsely into arse-cracks and cleavages.

More wise here, everyone wore their best—best patterns of
paint, that is—and otherwise nought but a sheen of oil and sweat
and a thin cord twixt their cunny-lips if they were women. Music of pipes, mostly of drums, had commenced gently early in
the evening, the drums first quietly insistent but building and
building in intensity the entire evening through, so that by the
time the party proper was begun they had become a pounding
rhythm that shook the very air we breathed and echoed in powerful synchronicity the pulse that beat within us.

Still rather new to the island and its ways, I was certain sure
that this was to be a night of novelties, and sensing early my own
significance to the feast, my loins entered into a state of constant
agitation, building a hollow chasm of subtle dread and excitement, chill and aching behind my warm and prickling mound.
My girls, having bathed me bade me stand and painted my body
with black, red, white and ochre markings symbolic of the stars
from which I had come—a different, poignant intimacy in the
painting sticks pressed gently on or stroking round my no-lon-
ger-private attributes and parts, forming concentric patterns
around my nipples and my slit.

Though I had known a similar occasion on which my body
had been hand-daubed white all over it remained a strange sensation, standing naked, a living artwork drying. For only when
dry and impervious could they brush onto me, with soft slick
brushes made of a tufted animal tail, the fine oil of their own dis-
tillation which made my skin shimmer in torchlight. Such exquisite caresses on such vulnerable places, for nothing was missed!
Then they placed upon my head the feathered crown with its
projecting penis decoration, draped me with a shimmering cloak

of exotic feathers that covered me entire, and finally presented me with the phallus-handled knife in the manner of a sceptre. The penis crown, I would later learn, was normally worn by male priests of the goddess to represent male virtues of strength and service. Slaying the old Black Devil had earned me this distinction.

Eight armed warriors bore me from the house, carrying me on a brand new litter, fitted with its own raised throne and draped with precious furs, all of which, I guessed, gave added elevation to both myself and to my status. As they bore me reverentially through the crowd there was not a man or woman who did not bow most humbly. At last they lay the litter down upon a brand new dais, upon which sat the thrones of our king and queen, my litter seat placing me only slightly below them. Arshon had drawn the line, it seemed, at elevating me above himself and his wife.

In front of the very same dais, where before the great stone had been, there was now a brand-new dome-shaped hut, sporting a huge crest of glittering feathers, and with two warriors guarding the curtained entranceway which faced toward the crowd.

As they had done at the wedding and as would prove usual at the commencement of any festival people were forming up into loose rows before the king and queen and seating themselves on the grass, listening to the music, talking to their companions and waiting for the celebration to begin.

It was I, it seemed, that they had been waiting for. Only moments after my arrival did the king rise to his feet and the whole assembly, including the musicians, fall silent. I would wonder if they thrilled to the sound of that voice as I did. Such strength. Such wonderful, manly warmth.

The detailed contents of Arshon's speech could not then be known to me and would only be loosely recounted to me months later as my knowledge of their language progressed, but in essence he welcomed them to a double celebration—to the celebration of the timely moon, and to the celebration of the famous slaying of the pig by a fertility goddess with hands become penises, ejaculating deadly thunder.

Several times within this speech Arshon gestured towards me, and every time he did so paused in speaking to allow a shout of what I would come later to recognize as approbation. However, since the sound contained some elements of ferocity and vengefulness toward the fearsome Black Devil, and was accompanied in many of those present by a quite frightening grimace of bared teeth, I—not knowing what was being said—found it most unnerving.

Towards the end of his speech, speaking in tones which seemed redolent of veneration, Arshon held out his hands to me, inviting me down from the dais, and the crowd roared again. I stood before him quite unknowing of what would follow, entirely vulnerable to his will, and the ache within me grew harder.

Reaching up, his expression sombre, even forbidding, he first carefully removed my crown and passed it to a servant who, with downcast eyes, placed it upon the seat of my litter. Then my king reached out to me again and gently lifted away my cloak, which was again transferred to the palanquin. T'was truly strange: I had lived entirely naked among them for what seemed a considerable time, by virtue of my office and status denied even the nubile thong which comes to women at marriageable age, yet the act of slipping the cloak from my painted shoulders felt so denuding, and the watchers reacted as if it were, with an audible gasp of excitement. I felt profoundly and vulnerably naked, there before them, as Arshon took my hand and, with a most enigmatic smile upon his darkly handsome face, conducted me into the hut.

In removing from me first my head-dress, which in symbolism I had regarded as the equivalent of a crown, and then removing what was clearly a ceremonial robe of some significance, I dwelt upon the ferocity and finality that had seemed to sound in his words and the shouts of the crowd and began to fret at the significance of it all.

In the dimly-lit interior beyond the heavily-curtained doorway I found my sweet June and Summer waiting, each seated facing forward, toward the door, at either end of the stone slab. Almost never before had either of them failed to greet me with a warm smile and thinking they looked both nervous and apprehensive I was further disquieted, wondering if it was this being enclosed in near darkness which discomfited them, their being separated the while from me, or some knowledge of theirs of what would follow.

Summer and June gesturing to me to sit between them I then did so, the stone very cold upon my buttocks, and they then gently took a hold upon me and folded me backwards across the block, so that my back rested on the stone itself and my head overhung the rearward edge of it.

Beyond the door I could hear a voice—perhaps Gorrogo's—and people chanting, whilst within the hut I could see not a thing at all, for whatever light there had been had been doused. I lay there, therefore, naked on my back, the stone abrasive on my back and arse, feeling somewhat chilled in the total darkness and wondering at the silence of my girls.

My skin prickled at that silence within the hut, for it felt so very portentous somehow. Nor, even after a while, did my posture feel much the more comfortable, for my head hanging of its own weight dragged down upon my neck and shoulders and my eyes, wide open, could see nothing but a blackness so threatening that I felt obliged to close them.

Then I felt a fleeting draught caress my legs and nether regions and, opening my eyes, glimpsed a faint lightening in the room, before the stygian darkness returned. I easily deduced, of course, that the curtain had been drawn and replaced, and the warm hands of my girls now took hold of my legs and lifted them upward, so that I lay horizontally extended, my lower limbs spread well apart.

And so different was this sensation, now, that I was truly sore afraid. I saw in my mind the almost sombre expressions of June and Summer, felt the hard coldness, un-cushioned beneath me, pondered anew the significance of the long painting ritual, and thought I must die. Both openings of my waste and sex in plain sight of the covered doorway and accessible to whoever had entered the room, what, I wondered, would follow? What would they insert, and where? A searing hot phallus? The blade of a knife?

Fear makes one foolish.

I remember catching my breath, emitting a long, slow, quiet hiss of surprise in the silent darkness as the first one found me.

Blind in the dark, like myself, whoever had entered the hut did so on his or her hands and knees and, oriented by a single glimpse of my mooning figure—for my arse lay as much off the rock as upon it—he or she must then have crept forward between my suspended legs. The first thing I felt, thus, was skin caressing skin somewhere about my inner left knee, and what might have been a nose first and then someone's gentle lips and tongue began tracing their way blindly along me, probing moistly along my thigh till I felt the face rest briefly on my cunny, the ebb and flow of soft, warm breath a gentle breeze whispering around my filling, tingling lips. And there I felt the face descend and, carefully, place a kiss upon both cheeks of my arse, darting left and right, ere the tongue lapped twice ever so briefly—little more than a kiss itself—at where the seeker supposed my clit to be.

That homage gently paid, he or she departed, twilight filling the chamber as the curtain opened and closed, then opened and closed again, to admit another. How many, I wondered, as I lay cunny upward on the great, chill stone, my ankles warmest in the grip of the girls who held them? All the men? All the women? And at the end, what then? Would they all be so gentle? Would this one, newly-admitted and striving blindly to find their way into me, to kiss me upon both arse-cheeks and somewhere in the region of my clit before departing, be gentle too?

Most were. As to how many there were, I frankly lost count.

Some, for whatever reason, began about my ankles, others seemed to find their way almost immediately to my arse, and every one kissed me just the one time upon each cheek before striving but briefly, with a lap or three of tongue, to pin-point my special, now very sensitive, focus.

As each seeker began, therefore, I knew not where he or she would begin, whether they would lick their way, or kiss, or guide themselves by soft-sliding cheek, and I never knew exactly where the two soft kisses would land, nor whether the third caress would fully find me.

Each time, then, began with a soft flutter of expectation. I would feel them work their way towards me, always softly, sometimes moistly, and wonder where the kisses would actually land—and what kind of kisses they would in fact be. Some were merely pecks, some withheld, however briefly, good mouthfuls of my cheeks. And the final kiss might be a moist brush of somewhere in the channel of my cunny, sometimes closer to that other hole than it, sometimes a little tickle of my gently swelling bud and sometimes, gloriously, a brief but lusty, thrusting-wetly, tonguing.

As seeker followed seeker, then, I gently began to writhe, the quite expected warmness flowing from the unexpected method, and within me a hunger long awakened, like a weary guardian warrior upon some threatened castle wall, grew sharper, more alert, made keener somehow by the swimming, fuzzy, dizzy warmth that occupied my heavy, back-tilted head.

And here an innovation, for just five seekers in I felt an unexpected, wonderfully familiar pressure lighting gently on my lips. By the light of the next flicker of the curtain I made out in the half gloom a beautiful and much-extended member, caught a wondrous man-scent in my nostrils. And in the fleeting light, too, a bright little gleam, a moist jewel in the small, dark eye of the penis.

Whose, I wondered? But I frankly scarcely cared. Thus invited, what could I do but take it, slick that first sweet moistness with my own? And the warm cock's unseen owner did not seek to draw him out, but rather moved a little nearer, slid him accommodatingly forward, plunged him sweetly deeper in my throat.

Oh wondrous largeness that forced my lips into that grasping

'O', that swelled my cheeks with the effort of containment, that beautiful hardness, smooth sweet slickness, soft recoiling to my gently questing tongue, curving like a pleasured cat, there to be nibbled, there to be teased, there to be wetly sucked.

And the lovely cock remaining throughout, I played the sweet instrument just as I was played, so that as my passions built I built the passion in it, and as my passions eased, so I gentled it away, in a process that seemed to me to last for hours.

And at the last, the final seeker stayed—held in place, I would one day be told, by my own lovely girls, who knew this seeker was the last and who knew that I was needing, and who knew the silent wanting of the owner of my cock, so that urged to bring me onward the seeker gladly did so, and allowed to bring my silent mouthful onward so did I. I found a glorious coming on my seeker's tongue, gushing long and sweet and wet, and brought that lovely cock quivering, gushing creamily into my mouth and throat, soft and slithering and filling.

A glorious wetness, in and out, it seems I must have nearly swooned and scarce remember being lifted from the temple hut to my throne upon the dais, to gaze in soft and joyful bewilderment upon the celebrations that were to follow.

Before us, now, began the games. Children ran races, warriors threw spears at a suspended target ring, fired arrows into the stuffed skin of a boar—the old Black Devil himself—and wrestled powdered and naked within a small enclosure, each endeavour cheered by their companions, or loudly and laughingly brought to friendly scorn.

The winners feted and cheered, the contest over, the village descended upon such provender as many in the world could only dream of, imbibing their soft warm ale and feasting upon such a vast range of delicacies, of fruits and nuts and fish and meats, that it would take too long to recount it.

I could scarce believe that the old Black Devil might taste this succulent, that fruits born of this earth could hold in them so very much of heaven, but all was pure delight when the girls began their dancing. What dancing!

Among our people corpulence seems entirely the province of individuals a little more than some two score years of age, and most of these are women. Childbirth, no doubt, plays a role in this, together with the fact that in the increasing family which ensues, children and young people rapidly assume the more energetic chores—the beach-combing, long walks in search of naturally occurring delicacies, transporting water in heavy gourds—so that a mother's life becomes easily sedentary. Corpulent men are rarer here—and far more rare than ever I found them in England—presumably on account of their being ever engaged in active friendly competition in some form or another and being energetic in their hunting and fishing pursuits.

The boys, girls, young people and those perhaps approaching middle-age (for the life-span here is four score years and more—much longer than our own) remain almost universally slender in form, and among them some so perfect to gaze upon that one could easily be moved to tears. There must be some similarity, one feels, between the lives of these people and those of the ancient Greeks, to explain the presence of so very many young and glorious Venus and Adonis forms.

Imagine a slender Venus, then, dancing surrounded by two-score matching siblings. Breasts like ripe, small fruit—full enough to be enticing and not yet heavy enough to drag—with their nipples ever on the upper curve, the curving cavity twixt and below their rib-cages is clearly defined and sinks softly ere it swells into the sweetly gentle mound of lower belly, the subtle rise whose poignant charm resembles that of the last low hill we climb ere we are home, its lower gradient carrying us swiftly and smoothly downward to the warmth and comfort that awaits below.

The simile must seem very strange to those who have not lived this life, in which one's gaze everyday in the course of the simplest, common events cannot but constantly alight, in their naked freedom, upon the parts of human bodies our world holds so privy and unmentionable. But here they know that cunny and yard and arse are as important to the whole as shape of face, or colour of eyes, that they are what—save in our gender—we all of us hold in common, are part of our human-ness, are lovely, sweet and clean.

Knowing no shame themselves, it is only the prurience of European eyes which, shocked at simple nakedness (and so hypocritical in that) would see wickedness in that dancing, of breast and buttock cheeks vibrating till they blur, of groins gyrating, hips swinging, bodies swerving, sinuous as snakes. Mouths smiling or softly grimacing at the pleasure of their own sensual freedom are open around white teeth and visible tongues, seeming to invite the presentation of clit, or tit or yard to them—but that's from untutored observation, mere impression. For having danced this way myself, being taught to do so by my girls, I know that there is no invitation in it until somewhere near the end. The dancer's focus, almost all the while, is in herself, and feeling herself watched and enjoyed she watches, feels and enjoys herself in a writhing, stamping recollection to herself of all that she can feel in every limb and sinew.

Then the men join in, having watched and lusted, and almost universally aroused, their movements somehow so aggressive, their buttocks hardening to the pounding of their legs, balls swinging, cocks upright, brisk and jostling.

Only at the end, hunger in men's eyes, weary with the dancing but yet not weary of it, a good fuck is but a lovely way to pursue continuance of the joy of dancing, the wakening of every sense and feeling, and bring it to a more fulfilling end.

Not all of them do, by any means, and most that do, do so with their man of choice, their husband or betrothed, whilst many have danced themselves to near exhaustion and subside upon the grass to be waited on by friends, family and as-yet-unrequited lovers.

My girls are among the dancers that night, always lead them at festival time, and I watch and am hypnotised by them. Their smiles are just for me, their bubbies and gentle mounds are mine, and I am stirring. The very memory stirs me still:

At last I am borne back to our dwelling, the curtain falls upon both our door and the village festivities, and I am weary, yet there remains that heat within me, burning slow as the embers of a well-kept fire and needing but a stir to spark and flame.

Juices of the entire adult population—or so it feels—moist and sticky on my arse and quim, June and Summer bathe me gently, yet differently, for it does not add to the languor in me, rather wakes and stirs me.

And stir me they do, too, smiling almost apologetically as they guide me to the love throne and then, to my mystification, bind me standing to its upright frame as Alfred bound me to his boat. I do not know, then, how much they place in hazard, handling a goddess in this way, feel only my naked vulnerability and its strangeness.

Then they produce my gift, and none could be the stranger.

It is a loincloth, made of rigid hide and suspended over the groin alone with cords that Summer tightly ties in the small of June's sleek back, joining to it there an under-thong that squeezes June's cunny and lies taut in the valley of her small round arse. Projecting through it at the front is a lovely cock-toy, a good man's hand-length long, thick and hard and upward curving.

To see my June with a man's erection quivering from her pubis, she a man with bubbies round and small, should, I think, be risible, but is not, and she is dancing, they are dancing, dancing to music in their minds alone yet which I can hear in the throbbing in my ears and temple, the pounding in my chest.

Their dancing dries my throat, seeks to draw me into it, makes my body want to dance, but it cannot, for I am bound, my arms and legs outstretched, my cunny open. And June is dancing the man's part now, dancing round the scourging trestle that Summer has slid into place, and I can see the him that June has become is lusting, wanting, the she who Summer is coquettish, spurning, teasing.

Now 'he' grabs 'her', wrestles with her, bunting her loins with the simulate cock, and now he turns and bends her, folds her over the trestle.

Suddenly submissive now, Summer hangs there much as she hung before to demonstrate the rapist's punishment, and I'm gazing at those sweet brown mounds and the peeping round eye with more fervour than I did that prior time, and my mouth is dry, a hard knot behind my pubis as June now suddenly strikes her.

She does not strike hard, she cannot, for she loves her, merely warms her lovely arse with impact heat. My body strains at its confinement, urging toward them, urging to stop them, urging to join them and still I cannot and I'm warm and wet, engorging everywhere twixt upper lips and lower.

Their dance become a playlet now, June lifts her, holds my Summer in a gentling warm embrace I cannot enter, and I watch their hands slide upon each other, caressing arms and shoulders, thighs and arse, Summer's fingers teasing the insensate cock, though you'd not know it was.

Subsiding to the ground before me they are kissing, completely melded one to another, breast on breast, belly on belly, and Summer's groping hand finds an oil flask and anoints 'him', and June the man now finds her, softly enters.

They play the lovers such that in my heated mind they are everything that they pretend and I watch the lips on lips of them, watch the smooth undulating rise and fall of June's own dear sweet brown bottom as she thrusts lovingly into Summer.

My whole body hard with straining now, I want them, my teats hurting in the urgency of desire, I am perspiring, feel an urge as if to piss that is sometimes the beginning, an aching heat of desperate wanting that roils and surges madly in my loins.

June's sweet small arse is bucking, both are moaning, and I close my eyes in my agony of wanting.

When I open them my lovely girls are standing, sweat-moist and smiling, and moving, praise the gods, now, soft towards me, till Summer, unreachable, stands before me, leaning forward, begins to suckle my breast. And June, behind her, is reaching around her, arms circling her bended waist, now drawing behind her and fastening the ties of the cock-toy she has relinquished.

Summer, now, at my lips and kissing, that gods-lovely wetness, caressing, deep-probing, my arms aching with wanting to hold her yet cannot, wrists hurting as they strain at my bind-ings, and a strange slick sensation between, now, my arse cheeks, for June is behind me, anointing. And the strangest sensation that makes me mew mutely into the mouth that suppresses my breathing, that I feel in the belly now pressed against mine as the false-cock is bunting my mound. I do not know the source of this, I cannot turn to see the string of beads that June is feeding one by one within my puckered, fluttering ring, that begin to fill me, inwardly touch me, rolling and bunting in mysterious places.

Summer's tongue now hard-pressing and probing inside me again I cry mutely as the cock-toy slides in me and fills me, and I feel now the thrust of her groin against mine, our sweat-moist flesh binding and peeling at contact and draw, and I feel the want building and I feel the dam breaking and I'm spilling, now wetly, my cunny and my arse full of glorious warm pressing—and now I am screaming, or would be. The gush and the breaking, the sudden great soaring that begins in my cunny, silently squeals in my arse as the beads are drawn, rolling, away in a rush, and my knees fail and I fall deep into warm darkness, at the near edge of madness in completed desire.

I begin to recover, untied, on our bed, Summer's arms round my breast, June's own round my thighs, and the whole world is spinning and I cannot stand, and I know nothing more till the morning.

So magical, was this. There was scarce a word that passed between us for want yet of language and yet our conversation continued quite endless, in looks and in touches, in movements of eyes and of limbs, of eyelids. Small gestures of hands and of fingers, were as eloquent now as any great orator's speeches. Hugs and embraces, stroking and petting and gentling and kiss-ing were restored to the purpose—it seemed—that gods or na-ture intended. We had few misunderstandings.

I was seduced, of course. So much beauty. So much gentle-ness. How could I not be? And learning so much to love what I had, I learned something else, too. I learned, now, to fear, for our safety.

Chapter the Tenth

In which I recognise defencelessness and meet with angels.

I f the Old Black Devil had done me a service in making of me a tribal hero, he was to do me yet another, for until that incident occurred I had given remarkably little thought to danger, arming myself only against the intrusion of snakes and biting insects.

The absence of warriors during the boar's incursion had also worried me, for I noticed it was no uncommon matter. Whatever it was that our fighting force did I never really did discover, for their seems to be something about the male psyche that needs to shroud in secrecy their collective acts away from home which is quite universal—but they were often absent. Part of this, I did establish, was to do with their fighting technique.

Although very rare it was not unheard of for canoe-loads of other islanders to chance upon our cove and land, there being very few other sheltered and accessible landing points about the island, and when they did so land it was our warriors' common practice to do no more than observe them from deep hiding. If the visitors minded their manners and contented themselves with seeking out some provender, taking fresh water from one of the many little streams, our warriors remained simply hidden, whilst if the new arrivals established a light camp this, too, was merely kept under observation. Only if it looked as if they'd intentions of staying would our fighting force then respond, initially by delegating one of their number to show himself, armed, at a distance.

If the foreigners responded by rushing him in a warlike manner or greeted him with a discharged arrow or a spear, and assuming that they missed him as they usually did, he would but run away and hide and our fighting men would remain where they were—for days, if need be, till the newcomers relaxed their guard. At this point our fighters would respond, usually by silently picking off small parties and individuals from the landed portion when they moved into the forest to look for food or to take relief. Not infrequently, either, our warriors would use their bows to pick off individual men about the enemy camp at night, disappearing into the forest again as soon as alarm was raised. They were so very good at this hiding and attacking that invaders never stayed, the gradual erosion of their company by forces they could neither see nor find no doubt playing havoc with their minds.

Ambush, then, rather than full battle, was our warrior's fighting method of choice, but it was potentially very costly and left the village, for all that it was concealed and approached by twisting ways, too often and too long exposed.

Because of all these things, on the rest day after the feast and having slept soundly from my earlier enjoyments and the later tender ministrations of my girls, I decided to call my own defences to account.

I was not afraid of guns. As a wilful and willing young associate of the huntin', shootin' and fishin' set in which my father moved I was never prepared to be a mere satellite and had set myself to learning all I could. In consequence I could bore you, my imaginary reader, with all sorts of facts and details regarding firearms (and fishing flies), but will not, save to reminisce about one favourite that I had and which, had I then been braver, might have taken my virginity.

Pistols were much the prerogative of men within my early life, though I was not alone as a girl and woman in learning how to use one, and it is hardly to be considered surprising that a wanton such as I should be intrigued by these other little yards, these members of brass and steel, their fiery, booming ejaculation and their solid, deadly seed. And of all my father's many guns there was one I really loved and wish I had kept with me.

Its style was a miquelet, its firing action clock-work, turned by a key, and its hammer reversed and falling toward the firer, but of more moment to me was its elegance. Moorish in style, beautifully filigreed and inlaid, its barrel was very long and very slender, externally thicker at one end and tapering smoothly to a lovely little fluted, round-lipped mouth. The pistol's grip too was surprisingly long, prodigiously curved, intricately decorated and tapered also, but at the lowest point of the hand-grip's taper it expanded into an elegant ivory ball about the size of a plum, an inverted Moorish minaret in shape like some sweet, small, perfect onion.

Is it to be wondered at that the girl that I was, whose wantonness seemed to spring from her pubis with its very first curl of maiden hair, sometimes, in the hottest days of summer, tickled my unseen, unknown bud with that sweetly graven chill of steel, or inserted that cool little minaret as far as it might go without my breaking?

But pistols, however delightful, have a single sore short-coming, especially that, indeed, of coming short, of lacking range. I had had to bring myself far too adjacent to the old black boar in order to be reasonably sure of putting a shot into him—and expecting to do so with my better hand—and I lamented that I had not, that morning, had a long musket prepared and made ready.

The thought, too, did cross my mind that I ought to train my girls or others in the use of these sophisticated weapons—their throwing spears and their arrows both having relatively little range as it was—but their reaction to my pistols seemed to make that quite impossible. Never having heard a shot fired the reports of my guns had filled them with the greatest dread and none had been able to even bring themselves to look upon me whilst I stood with a gun in my hand. That their goddess of fertility could control the thunder of heaven in her hands they could credit, but that they might do the same they thought not far from blasphemous.

Alone then, I decided to restore the rest of the late Alfred's guns to action. I had from the start made sure of their condition, taken all precautions to protect them from the climate by greasing them, packing them in oiled fabric and so forth. On investigation I found them not so much as flecked with rust but, in effect, in much the condition of new manufacture in which he had acquired them.

There were twelve of them in the case, all smooth-bore, flint-lock muskets, and all fully operable, and underneath them I found a shallow package of lead which, had I need of it, would add to my store of bullets. Sound powder—carefully cherished— I also had in goodly supply, together with flints and all other necessaries.

I kept just one musket at the house thereafter, very carefully concealed in the thatch, and the rest I moved, together with the main of my arsenal of powder and shot, to the menstruation hut I regularly shared with June and Summer. Looking after and occasionally practising with the weapons became a welcome break from my other godly duties.

And those duties I pursued assiduously and with little inter-ruption, day in, day out, for month after month, until—by my crude calculation—I had expended some four years on my is-land.

By this time I had encountered every form of ministration that would be asked of me, had been involved in every festival my people knew, could dance myself to a frenzy, and had learned to use their language perhaps more fluently than my own. This lat-ter brought me the greatest joy, enabled me to share much more of my people's thoughts and feelings and enabled me to share so much more of mine with my precious June and Summer.

I had learned to swim and met the sea-angels, learned to work the punishment stone and, to my unceasing joy, managed to con-vince my warrior clientele of the efficacy of a different—and for me far more enjoyable—style of blessing.

Hand masturbating our graduate warriors into a cup soon lost its limited appeal for me, save when I could use it to take one of them down a peg or two, and very often the surreptitious ex-change of their human milk for a modest mix of seed and firewa-ter seemed to teeter on the brink of discovery. I too often became alarmed, too much dreaded the task, and lost too much peace of mind on its account.

As soon as I had acquired sufficient language and understanding, therefore, I waited for one of those very infrequent nights of horrendous storms which, in my early days here, had truly frightened me. They happened neither frequently nor regularly, but they happened, and every time they happened Gorrogo and I were consulted as to which of the gods the village might have offended.

When the next real storm night came—not just a night of howling wind and rain but a night of cannon-like thunder and searing lightning—I announced the following morning that it was the mother-god who was displeased and that she had grown especially displeased with the graduation ceremony. My people, trustful and easily convinced, were full of consternation, until I told them that I had been instructed clearly in my dreams as to what changes I should make.

My invention, I'll allow, was far more fun to the wanton sprite in me, but would not be, I fear, to every conventional woman's taste.

Abandoning the box which my Mother Moon so disapproved of, I now greeted my graduates standing, embraced them and kissed them on the lips as they stood helplessly, wondering what on earth to do with their arms. Then I would bid them prostrate themselves on the bench, facing upwards, and, standing at their feet, I would watch, my expression forcedly enigmatic (you can have no idea how difficult it was to pretend such little interest), as my girls gently bound their charges into place. The Mother Moon, I told my captive warriors, required now that they did nothing but learn entire submission to her will.

On the slender justification that it was forbidden that the warrior should ever have the opportunity of looking down upon me, one of the girls then tied a blindfold over his eyes which both obscured his vision and bound his head to the bench. Memories of the sight of our warriors bound, blindfold, naked, helpless and erect, entirely vulnerable to whatever games we chose to play, stir me warmly yet.

Now, we stroked and touched the candidate's body with our three roving pairs of hands until he could not begin to know whose hands were whose, and I would then settle to teasing his cock, already upright, very, very gently with my hand.

Since I knew it gave them pleasure too, I allowed either June or Summer by turn to place themselves lightly on the warrior's upturned face and to occupy his mouth with her cunny. Not knowing to whom the cunny belonged, not knowing whom he suckled, such tremendous erections would result as to offer us the most wondrous pleasure. Shifting my own position and kneeling upon the floor beside his blind and naked body, some halfway between his head and waist, I would lean towards his towering, tumescent member and, carefully gauging with my finger on its pulse, breathe softly on the helmet of him, softly suck his engorgement in. Cunny in his mouth, his cock he knew not where, I would then begin to play with him in earnest with my mouth and tongue, desirous of both giving and obtaining the most prolonged pleasure I was able.

Within a certain time his cunny-muffled cries would reach a level of pleading that was far beyond resisting. Aroused by the feel of him inside my mouth, the caress of silken corded hardness upon my mouth-parts, and seeing June or Summer writhing ecstatically upon his desperate tongue whilst his own body threshed and bucked on the fur-padded bench like flotsam tossed in a storm wave, I would eventually give way and feel him coming, shooting wet and juicy into my mouth.

My cunny alive with the sear heat of my own desire, my skin tingling in every pore with wanting, I would then slide my come and saliva-lubricated mouth from off his member whilst the girl at his head slid off his face and gently removed his blindfold. And then the hardest part, best enabled by the kneeling position I have described which allowed me to pivot at the waist, bring my laden mouth from his cock to his lips, all the while seeking to keep his manly tincture contained and warm within my cheeks and not to swallow, until pressing my mouth to his and enjoining in a lovely, deep-throated kiss, I was able to present him with an equal share of his liquid white donation, commingling for both of us in the tastes of each other's mouths and the gentle lingering taste of that sweet cunny but recently withdrawn.

If any of these felt deprived of the searing whiskey-jolt conversion of which their predecessors reminisced, they never said so, and when I subtly made it known that Mother Moon considered the warrior braver and stronger who renewed his blessing from time to time (indeed we considered once a summer best), we gained no little extra business and no little extra pleasure. Warriors arriving for rededication and warm with memories of prior times presented often at the door with their cocks bulging enormous already and straining, so that it required extra effort on our part to prevent the ceremony from being a very short one.

I sucked their lovely, eager cocks, I played with them and kissed them, and it was wonderful to me, and no less so because my girls, excited, were swift to follow each occasion with 'Fucking Me Lady, Yes' and pursue it with a vigour born of their own so warm, wet cunnies and their wondrous, warm, free spirits.

Learning to work the punishment stone was a different matter entirely. Even before I had acquired very much of their language the girls managed to impress upon me that there were things my new vocation required me to know and to demonstrate without obvious assistance from them, and the punishment stone was one of these.

They led me quietly one time upon the left fork of the trail near my own stone predecessor, and which divided short of the home we called our menstruation hut. At the end of the trail was a most strange sight, set upon a small plateau on the top of a cliff, flanked on one side by the cliff edge and on three sides by a soft-stone ridge within which were the entrances to a number of pot-holes and small caves.

On a stretch of the trodden ground of the plateau, a number of wooden staples had been deeply hammered in. Each was made of the dark and extraordinarily hard wood from which their swords were made and which, being both relatively scarce and of an extraordinarily strong consistency, was highly prized. Regardless that it was extremely difficult to work—and perhaps even the more inspired by that inherent challenge—this timber was the island's common substitute for iron, of which they had none and was painstakingly and laboriously worked into the most exquisite forms.

Each of the staples was about a yard in length, some nine inches left protruding above the ground, and each, perhaps four inches across at the head, having a remarkable semblance to a giant embroidery needle, complete with its eye.

Seeing only the naked wooden pegs there I did not deduce their purpose until Summer lay down between four of them and June pantomimed tethering her spread-eagled body there, binding invisible cords around Summer's wrists and ankles, passing them through the needles' eyes.

The mental image of such defencelessness in the open air produced quite an astonishing effect within my loins and lower belly as I imagined myself bound in Summer's place as part, presumably, of some new, yet unexplained festivity. But there was nothing festive in the girls' expressions and I was not long in deducing the real purpose of the location and the restraining pegs.

Facing out to sea, in sombre echo of their expressions and the eerie nature of the site, stood what I first perceived to be a stumpy crucifix, some relic of missionaries long forgotten and for all I knew long-eaten, but which proved on closer inspection, in fact, to be a solid wooden pillory not at all unlike our own. Only, unlike any market-place pillory in my recollection, mildewed, worm-eaten human bones reposed at the base of this one.

They were ancient bones, I would discover, and the bones of a murderer from the village who, being divorced by his wife for physical cruelty, had decided no other would have her and slew her. He met the end prescribed for wilful murder and was bound to the pillory facing the sea until the gods—hunger, thirst and exposure in form—relieved him of his life. The punishment for rape I have recounted, and frankly I thought it very apt, and I had in fact been brought that day to the place of punishment.

At the time of my arrival on the island there was about the village one other known offender, who many, many years before had been found to have molested a child. In punishment they had cut his cock off, carefully so as not to kill him, embedded his hands in separate stones and bound his wrists to a wooden yoke that stretched behind his neck and shoulders.

Without means of escape, with neither hands nor yard to hurt others or to help himself with, his fate was a permanent disabling which left him entirely dependent upon others to keep him alive. When I arrived upon the island the victim of this criminal's actions was already a full grown, married man, the rare crime having occurred so long before, and the year following my arrival—on being besought at a public hearing—the former victim proclaimed his formal forgiveness. The stones and yoke were removed, but the length of time of the binding had rendered the limbs all but useless and the criminal became no less dependent upon the charity of others. June being excessively kind to him, he often came to her for feeding and for cleaning, but growing one day weary of his trial he merely walked off the edge of a cliff, and was never seen again.

Theft was almost non-existent as a crime and for good reason—the people had little enough to steal and for the most part a man coveting aught of his neighbour's need only ask and would be given or loaned it. With not a single braying ass upon the island still it was possible to covet your neighbour's arse, or his wife's or nubile daughter's, and whichever of them owned it would, as like as not, present it for your pleasure at your request. Yet rare as theft was, a punishment was prescribed, though this— like binding a murderer to the pillory—would not be inflicted by me, since it was not considered a sexual crime. Thieves had their hands stone-bound too, but this by custom was always only for a specified term of days. In fact I never saw it used upon a village man or woman, and I was soon to come to understand the dread that the stone—even were it to be worn only for a matter of hours—engendered.

Lest a punishment be required within my life-time I needed to be taught how to make the stone and apply it, and Summer had made a simple model pizzle for my initiation. She showed me how to pick and cut a reed to bind about and extend the cock, so that when the rock was made a pissing channel would remain, and then brought out of one of the caves some ancient urns of a kind no longer seen about the village. When their lids had been uncovered—oiled, stretched hide lay over them to keep any moisture out—I found one of the two urns she produced to be full of a grey-white powder, very soft in texture, the other full of small stones, pebbles and fragments of shells.

From the same cave, which contained a number more of the urns and a surfeit of additional pegs which some phlegmatic artisan must have carved to while away the hours, she produced one of several ancient moulds made from carefully bisected, and quite large, coconut pods. Placing the two halves of the mould around the model prong she showed me how the smaller hole at one end fitted around the balls of the man and how the reed which would make the pissing channel projected through the larger, upper, aperture. Wrapping the joined halves of the mould in a single sheet of hide and binding the whole together with tightly-knotted twine, she then produced a mixing bowl, a measuring cup, and a large gourd of water. She then explained to me the mixture, carefully accounting by drawing marks in the sand—so many cups of powder in the bowl, so many cups of pebble ballast added, all of it carefully stirred so many times, and then so many cups of water added-to, stirred very quickly and the mixture hand-scooped and firmed into the mould until it reached a mark on the rim. I noticed in particular how very frequently she mimicked the washing of her hands during the process of filling the mould and I wondered at its significance.

Two or three times she mimed or modelled the full procedure until I nodded comprehension, and after I had demonstrated it in a similar mime to her I then proceeded to make a stony cock-weight around the toy. At the end I knew confidently how to carry out the task and understood the better, perhaps, why crime here was so very rare.

Learning to swim was another matter.

By the time I was married I think there was little a civilised society had to offer which I had not at some point tried, and after a
very few weeks on the island it seemed to me that there was little
'uncivilised' society had to offer that I had not attempted also.

From early on, however, whilst being bathed by my lovers in
the stream, I observed them and others of our people swimming
in the lower and deeper reaches of the waterway, and this I admired and envied, never having learned that skill myself.

Summer one day having clearly glimpsed my depth of longing, invited me to join them with a tug upon my arm and a warmly beckoning expression on her face. Seeing me draw back in
anxiety — the deeper water was really rather near — an astonished
expression appeared on her face. Drawing me carefully aside, as
if concerned we might be seen, she pointed at me, briskly mimed
the act of swimming, then gave me a deeply searching look. Feeling vaguely embarrassed, I shook my head, and was frankly both
surprised and a little unnerved at the look of grave anxiety which
appeared on her face.

But a little while later and after whispered conversation twixt
the two, Summer and June led me quietly away, fetching with
them — somewhat unusually — the two guards from our hut. Proceeding along a path that showed every sign of being long un-
used they eventually stationed our guards upon it and led me on
some considerable distance alone, bringing me eventually to a
distant part of the beach where virgin sand gave way to stands of
littered rock and myriad rock-pools of all shapes and sizes.

In these, then and there, they taught me to swim, spiriting
me frequently away to this secretive location thereafter, to make
me proficient through practice. And there can be, I must admit,
few more enjoyable pastimes than being taught how to swim by
two lovers.

There's the immediate shock and delight of transition from
balmy air to the first strike of what seems such chill cold wetness.
One's nether lips close as an oyster to protect their precious pearl,
until acclimatised, and then there follows that wondrous feeling — the caress of water on her and smooth betwixt one's legs,

softly probing and stroking those places only lovers and mothers have touched before.

To wade as I in my youth had waded, clothed, into a stream, and feel the fabric of one's clothing clinging clammy, chill and damp, gripping or clumping in awkward, uncomfortable places, filling here and there and ballooning out with air, threatening too oft to overthrow one, has no comparison whatever with this thrill, with this soft glissage of water unfettered over naked skin, with the wondrous sense of oneness with the all-but-invisible medium which supports us.

And ere it did support me June and Summer did, their gentle arms strong around me, under me, touching soft and lifting me, bearing me safely and intimately in warm caress until I learned to trust that water can do likewise. What a joy that is, to slide through space, tiny bubbles streaming, and when you can descend—as I soon could—beneath the water, what treasures there, of glittering fish, glowing coral and shimmering fern.

Resting at times I then could watch my darlings from close quarters, poems of gleaming brown curves cleaving smoothly through the water, feeling it caress them as intimately as I so loved to do, watching it gleam as diamonds upon them as they emerged into the sun. What a pleasure, too, to sit in water grown comfortably warm, the expiring, kissing slap and lap of waves upon your bubbies, fingers or toes playing beneath the wetness in the wetness within my lovers, even as their toes and fingers play in mine, whilst myriad jewels of tiny fish cluster about our limbs, somehow seeming to find sustenance in our skin, and tickling so sweetly.

It made sense to me eventually, that their goddess of fertility should be native to the water, and at this early time I was surprised that no one challenged, no one queried my deception. Perhaps it was that June and Summer had already either come to love me or in some way to like things as they were, sufficiently to choose to collude thus with me, but this I did not know.

Surrounded by the sea, they considered water the source of all the world's life and nourishment. Unable to drink seawater they believed that the clean drinking water of the streams was drawn from the sea and carried to the land as rain. Tree roots, too, which they saw only in their upper reaches or in those waterside species whose roots may themselves run into the sea, they believed to percolate down through the whole of the land, finding the sea and its water beneath.

My arriving in a boat might have disabused them, save that they had never seen a vessel like it nor so provided for, and thus in their reality and myth it became the chariot of my delivery, the mechanism for bearing my gifts. Such, of course is religion, capable of almost any accommodation, and I might have floated naked from the sky on wings of parchment and they would still have named and used me as they had.

The crucial importance of swimming, I learned at a feast that marked the beginning of our season of plenty, a different diversion from the rest. Setting aside, that day, my litter, I was collected by a group of warriors that morning, lifted aloft and bodily borne along between them, much as I had been upon the night of my arrival.

Gorrogo, the king and queen preceding us, the entire village following on behind and many heavily laden with baskets of fresh fish, we walked for much of the morning along the beach, coming eventually to a beautiful little cove, and here I was set gently down facing out to sea. I wondered why, wondered what could or would be expected of me here.

Everyone else, now, was standing some yards clear behind me, save inevitably for my two girls who stood beside me and began to walk forward into the water, pressing gently at my elbows to indicate that I should advance too. The water but halfway up to my knees we stopped, the girls in turn stepping in and turning to face me, then lowering themselves to their knees in the water, holding to me and taking a 'blessing' from me that made my knees vibrate.

Already aroused by the strangeness of the situation, at being tongued by June and Summer in full view of the adult population of the village, I was somewhat startled when Summer, rising second, surreptitiously yet firmly smoothed my pubis and my under-parts with a gesture of her palm and fingers, then straightened-up smiling very gently and faced with me back out to sea again.

I did not look — for I could not mistake the secrecy in her gesture — but I could feel something rather nastily sticky, slick and oily lying thickly there upon me, oozing thicker than semen on me from quim to arse and twixt my upper thighs, whilst from it I caught an odour not altogether unfamiliar in that region, but altogether stronger than any I had known.

Advancing toward the sea again the girls placed firm and gentle hands upon my forearms, the gesture gently reassuring — and it needed be. Cleaving toward us was a silver blue fin and I thought with terror 'Shark!'

And I'd recognised that smell as well and couldn't believe what they had done, what my lovely, loving Summer had done! Could anyone be capable, in truth, of such a terrible treachery? Or was I about to die, the casualty of some false superstition, some act of folk-lore which — inconsequential to a god — would be more than consequential to the mortal that I was? I almost swooned I think, in my distress and helpless horror, imagining the razor jaws enticed by the glutinous paste of fish so slick between my legs slamming tight upon my arse and cunny and dragging me screaming beneath the water! I closed my eyes in shock and horror.

Instead I found something bunting at me, prodding at me like an overlarge, rather stubborn and over-hungry penis. Opening my eyes in puzzlement I saw a vast array of teeth and a cunnilinguist's fantasy of tongue, beneath eyes that seemed to sparkle with amusement. The mouth was curved in an endless smile, and a sound emerged like a softly fizzing, clicking chuckle. I was being cunny-nuzzled by a dolphin.

Applauding villagers advanced to the water's edge and threw in gifts of fish to the waiting dolphin tribe, laughed and clapped to see them at their play. I do not know when it began but for many years, I would come to learn, they had been giving them these gifts of fish during the dolphin's mating season and the dolphins seeming to have come to expect it now rewarded them with their play. 'Twas the first time, though, that the villagers had brought a living goddess with them, the first time a dolphin had kissed her there, and, that first time, I could not but wonder idly if my dolphin was a boy.

One came to know the difference soon when one swam naked among them as Summer, June and I did then and for many another season. Never have I known a more sweetly sociable species—the aquatic equivalent of my people, yes, but my people are exceptional—and the dolphins' visits are always completed too soon. And lest I might leave you wondering, yes, the male dolphin is equipped with a most wondrous, prodigious yard and it feels exquisitely delightful in the hand.

Summer's secret blessing of my cunny in order to entice the dolphin, my secret swimming lessons too, illustrated this strange collusion which seemed to have grown between us. I was unfailingly treated by every village member, my lovely acolytes too, as the very incarnation of a goddess, and yet, in private, I could not but wonder at the miraculous accommodations to which my beloved girls were party. I had no means to tell them, now, of my feelings and my gratitude and could therefore only do the strange things that they asked of me. And with every incident they seemed less strange, which sometimes affrighted me too.

In such moments of reflection as I had, half-full of self-accusation and recrimination, still the recent memories of such happenings would flood my groin with unaccustomed warmth and yearning, till I felt my bud glistening, peeping and wanting and ached all the more for the next.

Chapter the Eleventh

In which the Devil wears a human face.

A s my wondrous new life proceeded it seemed to me often a miracle that I sustained it. Never, save perhaps when my lovely Sam was weaving spells with his wand inside her, had I ever thought my cunny to have magical properties, and it stood to reason—in my view—that over time my failures should undermine my people's belief in me, and yet it was not so.

I appeared to have successes—dear Minnarra had a son, and that first much pregnant woman had the male child that she wanted, whilst all my graduate warriors would come to boast of my having turned their very milk to liquid fire, or of having kissed their very prowess into them, invigorating and empowering them. Gorrogo—who could so easily have been mine enemy—became and remained a close and trusted friend and ally, and not a one of those who cunny-kissed and sucked me ever approached me to lament it.

The small man with the large wife would return to me every so often for renewal and—presumably enlivened by the taste and scent and heat of me—would go away inflamed with passion and sustain his woman for some while, even producing a child in result. The rapist, too, was oft returned to me for his carefully considered punishment and I never lost the fervour of my fury. The girl herself becoming satisfied the punishments lessened over time and eventually she freed him from the rope. Several years would pass, though, ere the council freed him from his groin weight, so that he long remained dependent upon the kindness and tolerance of others.

Wherever the flame of desire in a couple's marriage reduced to embers, the ministrations of my cunny in the presence of my acolytes frequently proved at least temporarily incendiary, and my girls themselves, however gently, did teach some men and their wives certain necessary and intelligent variations in their sexual techniques. And chance alone dictated that others who came to me in earnest of the birth of a son or daughter would receive the child that they wanted, whilst those who did not found a purpose in the failure. It was a commonplace for such to thank me for the greater wisdom I had shown in not producing the wanted sex and in causing them to re-think the issues which had brought them to that choice.

Since fucking was—rather wonderfully—both everyone's tribal and social duty and their principal means of pleasantly whiling away spare hours, it was likely, too, that she who did not produce the wanted sex this time would do so in the future, so that no-one ever seemed to give up hope or sustain more than a temporary irritation (never addressed to me, for fear of punishment) at my 'failure'. There would be odd demonstrations of disappointment, but Summer and June would mitigate the matter in their careful, lovely way.

There were some notable failures—a young man and an old whose flaccid members must remain so, however we teased and played. The old man shrugged, the young man wept, and in both instances my Summer and June were very much their comfort, holding them, talking with them, confiding with them.

To each of them they introduced the wooden cock, making each a gift of one from a developing supply provided by the chair-maker, who as their master-craftsman had made them for Gorrogo, and who had them made, now, for me by the very same apprentices who'd acquitted my throne's engraving.

Whilst anyone could obtain these simulated yards, they were considered entirely valueless until and unless they had been blessed by Gorrogo or, latterly, myself. The form of his blessing I neither know nor care to dwell upon, whilst mine was to have them carefully introduce their carven appendages to my inner wetness before giving them suck on she whom they so valued. And to my gain, before that artificial penetration and my blessing, the two men were carefully taught to use the device well and, introduced by June and Summer to the anatomic model, were taught and shown how to bless their women with their tongues before, to my early astonishment, being offered practice on the girls themselves.

How very strange it was for me to witness that—my Summer squatting upon the face of an ageing man with a petrified cock, being licked and sucked by him, him listening to her reactions, learning from her pleasure, and June, too, upon the youth whose cock hung cruelly bent and broken, each time with the girl not being tongued leaning close, encouraging, advising.

When thus the men graduated to their goddess, me, their eager, lusting, wanting tongues and the instruments of pleasure they had been given were presented, however gently, schooled and practised, and it was I who reaped the benefit.

And each left happy! A cock not their own to bless their women with, my own wet blessing smearing their faces, and each condemned to a wanting forever, or so it seemed to me.

And such was my routine, then, for much of the time I was with them, trading my blessing tacitly for my sustenance and their affection, helping men and women troubled by issues of fecundity, sexuality and the characteristics and beliefs which they attributed to them. And all, essentially, remained happy. The numbers of supplicants reduced over the ensuing months and years, making the days pass easier, the villagers were well-satisfied with what they believed that I did for them and, thanks to the frequent ministrations of my two young acolytes and their subsequent replacements, I was myself kept satisfied and largely free of wanting.

Some ten years into my sojourn, by my islanders' accounting, much remained the same, I persisting in my duties to the people of our community, they persisting in their own duties to me, and all of it with much happiness. The population had grown and warrior cocks remained in good supply, together with the various other supplicants for my special blessings which have already been described. I had been cunny-kissed by countless dolphins, been tongued many times in the warm darkness of the Mother Moon Celebration Temple, and had on each of those occasions enjoyed that anonymous yard in the darkness. My skin was not so white as it had been, but if anything my hair (all my hair) was fairer, and that upon my head tumbled in reckless abandon a long way down my back.

My lovely Summer and June, in time, were wedded, June in about our fourth year, Summer in our sixth, three further acolytes had come and gone, being replaced in due course by Butterfly and Tandi. My domestic arrangements became somewhat changed, a private inner sanctum being built within the house, and I shared my bed every night with Butterfly and Tandi, and often with my former acolytes, continuing my lovers, too. They so loved to play their games with me and enjoyed me no less than I enjoyed them, allowing me to pleasure them in the ways they had so often pleasured me. I have worn the loin-cloth cock and pleasured them with it, fucked my lovelies with it and been fucked with it wondrous often myself, have learned to feed beads into a lover's arse, and when and how to withdraw them, have laughed with them and cried with them, held my Summer's baby in my arms.

I looked younger then in the hand-glass from the toilette set than I would have supposed, owing largely, I think, to long rests in the shadows out of the burning light, the most delightful sex life I have ever known, and a feeling of general ease which permeated my mind and body. Being so much loved, I think, still kept me very young.

But those ten or so years later—by the calendar of my people—there came a day of horror worse than anything they or I had ever known, the arrival of a Devil far worse than him whom I had slain, and far more dangerous than ever that pig could have been. Nothing would ever be the same again.

I was walking, daydreaming, in the humid coolness of the forest, when the sudden, frightening sound of shots intruded upon my languor and sent me rushing toward the village. Either someone had accidentally discharged my guns or the worst that I had grown to fear had finally occurred.

It was the latter.

Choosing a careful vantage point I gazed down into the village. My having previously persuaded Arshon of the danger of the whole warrior force leaving the hamlet undefended, a small body of guards had been left to defend it whilst the main force went off to do whatever it was that they did. Of the eight men in that guard contingent one lay still and lifeless on the grass, another was crawling painfully away, and the remaining half dozen had cast down their spears and stood rooted to the spot.

Occupying the centre of the village some twenty foreign, well-armed natives formed a very crude circle around the area where sat the thrones and cleaving stone, whilst within that circle stood a half-a-dozen men who were clearly European, and all of those equipped with guns and swords.

It was that half-dozen which made the difference. I knew our warriors would soon be here, if they were not already and watching from hiding, and I knew that they could well dispose of the score of blackguards in the circle. But against a dozen firearms and more—for most of the white men wore at least two pistols and carried a musket besides—I knew they must fare badly. I could even see that one of the ruffians had a pepperbox in his belt—a gun with six rotating barrels, each charged with a separate shot.

I could fetch my guns from the menstruation hut and begin to pick them off, but I knew they would hardly sit still for that and being almost certainly wise enough not to charge blindly up at me and give hidden warriors their advantage, 'twas far more likely that the people in the village would be used as hostages, that a massacre would ensue to provoke our men into a vain attack.

Already I was aware of one of my girls nearby me and a warrior crawled into place beside us. The girl I charged to find another and to fetch my guns from our menstruation hut, lest guns might prove to be of use, then I bid the warrior find his captain and deliver to him my suggested plan.

'Twas then I saw two white men from the inner group rush out, towards one of the row of houses whose entrances faced away

from me and which included my own, and drag back with them
a woman—my own, my precious Summer. Drawing the terrified
girl within the ring they presented her to one man whose garb,
despite two pistols in his belt, was clearly that of a priest. And
now I saw that they had conducted a rapid search of the place,
for he was brandishing the wooden carving of myself before her,
and in his other hand he gripped the punishment whip.

He was screaming words at her, unintelligible to me and almost certainly so to her, and I could see her vigorously shaking
her head in mute incomprehension. The bastard tucked the whip
in his belt and slapped her twice, still shouting, the sound of the
slaps like shots in the overpowering stillness. Still she did not answer, for in truth she could not answer, did not know his tongue.
He drew his arm a long way back and delivered another slap
which cast her to the ground, then summoned a man from the
defensive ring whose subsequent gestures, posture and action
proved that he had been summoned to interpret. Whatever the
question was this time she clearly understood it, I could read the
fear in her cowering posture, and I saw her shake her head, knew
this time that it was a blank refusal of compliance.

The priest-type bellowed, barked an order as he pulled the
whip again from his belt, and two of his men laid filthy hands
upon her. The moment they dragged her to the stone and drew
her over it, the priest raising the ugly five-tailed lash above the
curving glory of that lovely arse, I knew I could delay no longer.

"Who are you scoundrels and what do you want?" My voice
rang loud and clear, causing all of them to turn. The priest-beast,
to my relief, lowered the vicious whip and bestowing upon me
the most baleful, venomous stare hissed:

"What god-forsaken bitch of whoredom have we here,
lads?"

"I am no harlot!" I declared; "Only a castaway, late of the Talisman, being cared for and protected here."

"Cared for and protected? Cared for and protected!" The repetition came with explosive force: "D'ye expect me to believe that
thou walks't naked here among these heathen, that ye're recog-

nised in this graven idol found among th'most outrageous carvings and utensils, and yet art not a harlot!" Again the final words
came almost as a bellow of indignation. He hissed:

"Hussy! Trollop! Brazen harlot! That is what ye be, as sure as
t'was our vengeful God as brought me here!"

He was an ugly man, and smelled like the others, of urine,
old foodstuffs, dirt and grease, and he wore a tonsure on his high
round head such that, to my mind, his dark hair ringed it like
a foreskin. His head looking like a penis, he probably had the
brains of one. At least, I hoped as much.

"Take her!" he shouted, and I was grabbed, and dragged—to
the cleaving rock, even as Summer was pulled aside. The men at
my arms dropped grinning to their arses, scraping my bubbies
and my belly on the rough stone as they dragged me forward
over it, my arse waving helpless in the air.

"Filth!" he screamed, and I could have screamed too, as the
five braids smote upon my cheeks. "Wanton, loathsome, filth!"
he bellowed, and striped me yet again, only the greatest will on
my part keeping me quiet.

"STOP!"

The voice was the voice of command, was Arshon's voice,
speaking English to someone other than myself for the first time
in his life. He had asked to learn it and had been taught, but none
but he and I had ever used it.

"This wog speaks English!" one of the ruffians averred; "Now
wot d'yer make of that!"

"Let my wife alone!" Arshon commanded; "And tell me what
you want!"

He'd stilled the whip, and stilled my heart in calling me his
wife, however falsely, but I knew he would not hold them back
for long.

"Your wife is it?" the priest responded, sneering: "A white
woman and a blackamoor, and nary a church in sight? I think
not!"

I felt, somehow, the rising of the whip, heard Arshon demand
again:

"Tell me what you want!" and I answered for them, addressing the grass which, my arse in the air, remained only inches from my face:

"They want the gold, my lord!"

That had their interest, and no doubt his, since gold was here unknown. The priest spoke as if he knew that:

"There's no gold on these islands!"

"Not of our ground or excavation, that's true," I answered; "All the treasure here is found."

"What treasure?"

Beneath the disbelieving tone I heard his greed. I knew I had his interest, and I answered:

"The further side of the island. The coast is rough there, and two ships in past times were foundered on the rocks. There was nought but a small chest in one, but the other must have been a treasure ship of sorts."

Had I spoken of only a single ship and that a treasure ship I know he would have believed the simpler lie the less. Why would I embroider the tale with such an unnecessary detail if what I said was not true?

"You seen this ship?" he demanded sharply.

"'Twas rotted away long ere I came here, but I know where they buried the stuff."

"Buried? You mean to tell me this midden of fuzzies here found gold and gems and yet there's not a sign of it upon them? Fuzzies who'll sell their brats fer a set o' glass beads?"

"They're not like the rest," I answered truthfully enough, then; "'Tis their way to think it wrong to steal from the dead, unless they've killed them in battle themselves, and to bring any of the treasure here would be to bring bad luck."

The priest pursed his lips, veered onto a different tack:

"Where's his warriors?"

"What?"

"This wog chief. Where's his warriors?"

"Hiding in the forest," I answered truthfully.

"So if we go looking for this treasure they'll be on us," he mused aloud, the question implicit.

"He will call them in if you promise to take what you need and go."

"Will he, though?"

I could see the nasty smile in the back of his eyes. I knew what he was thinking, the lies he was planning, the murders and rape that must surely follow, and I naked, arse in the air and exposed, with two grinning bastards pulling hard on my arms. I answered firmly:

"He will if I ask him."

"You are his wife, then."

"Yes." Oh to have said that word! Even in pretext!

The midden-reeking irreverend pondered, then:

"Tell him."

I said, looking straight at Arshon: "Please; call in the spears!"

There was no sign in his face that he'd understood, detected my gentle emphasis, yet after the briefest pause, his expression as if he were about to refuse, he sighed defeatedly, turned and hailed the forest in our own island tongue:

"Spearmen to me!"

We watched the warriors warily emerge. Penis-head demanded:

"How many?"

"About 40. There are fifteen more at a camp at the further end of the island, but they'll not even know that you're here yet."

"They'll have heard the guns!"

"And they'll think them mine—that pair you're wearing—for I hunt with them often enough."

"You've not many fighters for a village this size." Perhaps he was not as stupid as he looked. I answered bitterly:

"We've never needed many."

Three white men and ten brown were left to watch the village, the remainder embarking on our walk to the far side of the island. I was stark naked still, made for the first time in my island life to feel soiled by the very gaze of men, and my hands were tied painfully tight behind my back, above my buttocks. Penis-head walked directly behind me and kept pushing me with the head of the whip. Every so often he would flick my arse with it sharply to remind me that it was he who was in charge.

The change occurred very quickly, a sudden sound somewhere twixt a hissing and the raising of a flock of birds, and all around us his warriors stumbled and fell. All but one of the natives dead, the priest and his two companions found themselves entirely surrounded by warriors with drawn bows. Our fifty archers, you see, knew already of my swiftly whispered, half-thought plan, and would anyway have been insulted if they'd thought the call for spearmen included them, so they had watched us coming, and knew what they must do.

"Surrender," I told the reeking reverend; "or they will kill you here and now."

Three white men captured, the brown warrior slain where he stood, we re-crossed a part of the island to the bay, needing now to know how they'd arrived. We found two long-boats on the beach and six guards—two of them Europeans—and we saw a ship, too—presumably their own—hove-to some leagues distant from the shore because the tide was low.

Evening was already drawing in and the tide would soon turn, but in the low light and at such distance from the ship I knew the boat guards could not be clearly seen. Save the three archers who stood with knives at our prisoners throats every other man fired at a word and the men on the beach toppled almost as one, quilled like parodies of hedgehogs.

Seating the dead in attitudes of rest, removing two of the natives and leaving two of our own in their place who could run to us with alarm should the ship put another boat out, we attended to their brethren, who had neither heard nor seen a thing, just a little after night fall.

Despite their hostile occupation—for I reckoned them pirates and slavers—the dissipated followers of the villainous priest—who called himself Padre Cacopardo, though his accent was as common and English as any heard around Tyburn's gallows—were no match for our warriors. Twixt the prowess derived, perhaps, from kissing my cunny and the long periods they had spent in our forest, our men were fleet, strong, silent and, above all accurate.

But not all the killing was swift. I saw some cruel treatment of the brown men, many among our number seeming to bitterly resent their giving service to what they now knew must be a foreign white race, and I must confess to a quite naïve astonishment and distress at the pleasure some of ours took in inflicting pain on theirs.

Such is always human vengeance, it would seem, when fanned to flames by deep contempt and anger. The screams and cries I heard that night were the stuff of nightmares, so alien did they seem to what I had known and seen here, yet none of the screams were so haunting as that of the one white man at the village who, having killed a woman of ours out of hand, died slowly and shrieking after ours had lopped his cock off.

Without a gunshot fired since shortly after their arrival and with no alarum sounded, their mates on ship had seen no cause for intervention and the first they knew of their disaster was when, the following morning, we set fire to their boats and laid out the bodies of their dead on the shore. Unable to close-to, the ship sent another, smaller boat in timid reconnaissance, and as soon as they were close enough to see the measure of our success a score of our warriors, laid upon the ground and absolutely terrified, fired a single ragged volley with every gun we had. My musket alone found a mark and sent one sailor sprawling, but the show of force was sufficient to dissuade them.

The ship stayed only until nightfall when, seeing no sign of our moving, and reading, perhaps, a greater power in that volley than we ever had, she departed under lantern and was never to plague us again.

Taking stock of our situation was very, very painful.

The first white people my own people had set eyes upon other than myself were this crew of malodorous, vicious ban-

dits—though the villains called their business 'trading'—and I
was sure that this encounter must perforce affect my congregation's attitude towards me. Yet if it did I saw no sign of it. Though
Summer had felt their hands upon her, and another had fondled
Tandi's tiny breasts, none of my girls—I thank Heaven—were seriously hurt or considered themselves so, and you can perhaps
imagine my joy when all of them, Summer at their head, rushed
to encircle and embrace me.

Five of ours had the bastards slain, and a score of our women
they had laid hands upon—besides myself—in a manner considered indecent. The swift conclusion of their invasion, as it seemed
to them, and the peculiar deference of the men to the quasi-re-
ligious prejudices of their leader, had prevented these molesta-
tions from descending into rape so that all were but touchings
and fondlings, yet to touch any woman without her consent was
to our people no less a crime.

Like much of the village I stood, still in the embrace of Summer and Tandi, and gazed upon our captives who, tightly bound,
were laid in a line upon the green, presently un-molested except
for being frequently spat upon. Including the 'priest' we had six
captives, of whom only one survived from the native party, and
all save the priest showed every sign of terror.

Summoned to the king's house I found the council in ses-
sion—the king himself, five men and five women, Minnarra
included in their number—and found them earnest but not un-
welcoming. Arshon smiled at me—his smile a little tired—and
indicated that I should join them. Minnarra embraced me tightly,
her eyes moist with tears. Because the offences included molestation, my presence was entirely usual.

"It is our belief," Arshon told me quietly in the language of
our people; "that these strangers should be punished in accordance with our law. Because they are not of our own kind and
others might come later, we wish to know if you would counsel
otherwise."

I shook my head, answering;

"The speedy resolution to which matters, my lord, were

brought, cost us four brothers and a sister killed, and a score and more molested. Had the resolution not been speedy I can promise you of a certainty that our losses would have been much worse. These men have the look of slavers and would, I'm sure, have killed very many and taken others into a forced labour they would never have escaped.

What the council does to them is for the council to decide, and I'm sure thy thoughts do tend to these villains' execution. There is nothing I could or would choose to say in mitigation of their evil, I would only counsel that when 'twas done all trace of all of them should be removed and the memory of the day be slain by silence."

Arshon nodded and, within a few moments, the matter was decided. The molested must have their grievances requited, the dead avenged. As a victim myself, and fluent in their tongue, it was decided I should tell them.

Chapter the Twelfth

In which the very devil comes to kiss a Lady's cunny.

The village assembled around us, the king announced his decision, pausing after every few words that I might make translation. The bound and hobbled prisoners were raised to their feet and held supported by two warriors apiece in order that the crowd could gaze upon them, and I stood before the party's erstwhile leader, addressing my words directly to his loathsome face. What I translated was this:

"I Arshon, your chosen king, make known to all the will of the council and the people. The act and intent of this raiding party was to murder and to plunder. Five of our number were rubbed out by their actions. For this we make no distinction in guilt between the prisoners. Finding all of equal guilt, we are determined all will be equally punished. The punishment is death."

But for the support of the warriors one of the prisoners would have fallen, his knees buckling, a plaintive, barely human wail escaping twixt his lips. The king proceeded:

"Sisters of our family were molested, indecently touched, and our own high priestess of Mother Moon was violated in an act of blasphemy."

I enjoyed the look on Cacopardo's face as the import of those words sank in, as he realised how they regarded me and that at this moment, in my pagan nakedness, there was greater power in my hand than his. Arshon concluded:

"Immediate death does not requite their blasphemy, nor their molestation, and thus it is decided that prior to their execution each one must know the burdening."

I could see the perplexity in the faces of the men, their fearful incomprehension, and I was not of a mind to enlighten them. Arshon ordered: "Begin!" and several of our men stepped forward, each one brandishing a knife.

Cacopardo remained silent, but few of the others did, bab-

bling and pleading in their terror, falling silent at least briefly
when our people's purpose became known, cutting and strip-
ping the clothing from our captives' bodies and finally cutting
the hobble in order that they might walk.

It was at that moment that, by some inordinate effort—unless in their contempt for him the guards had slackened their
hold—the native prisoner tore himself away from his immediate
captors, threw himself onto his knees before me and began to
kiss that part of me which was nearest to his lips, the gold-curled
muff above those lower lips of my own. Betwixt his passionate
but sadly misplaced kisses he babbled continuously, imploring
the mercy of the "Goddess of the Moon".

As the guards moved swiftly towards him Arshon stayed
them with a gesture, announcing:

"In our contempt we do acknowledge the servile nature of
our coloured brethren, commanded to their part by order of their
own kings. This man has not molested women here and makes
an offer of fealty to her we love." I did not fully comprehend
his meaning but could see many villagers nodding. Then Arshon
asked me quite directly:

"He gives himself to you, and we are glad to honour his gift:
will you spare his life and take him as your slave?"

There was much to warrant discussion here, but I sensed what
all were wanting and that that in part was an act of magnanimity
to balance out the harshness of the day. For my part I could see
his terror, knew his presence on the island was not truly of his
choosing, and could not but help observing to myself the patent
quality of his yard. Thus I accepted. He and it—within whatever
circumscribed use I could make of either—became mine.

I coaxed him gently from the ground, his dampening chin
in my palm, nodded toward his face and offered the tight, bitter smile which was all that I could muster. Rarely have I seen
a look of such joy and gratitude upon a human face outside my
temple.

Our five convicts, then, naked as the day they were born, save
in the matter of bodily hair, and hands bound tight behind them,

were marched in close procession to the place of punishment. Upon our way, of course, we came to the stone statue of my previous incarnation and here the column paused. In response to Arshon's words I turned to the captive leader:

"That piece of stone, Cacopardo, is me. The king commands that you bow down and kiss my cunny." I knew he would refuse. I hoped he would refuse.

"Ye'll not see me bow to gods of stone, you filthy wanton, and I will die a thousand times ere I will bow to one of thee!"

"I hoped you would say that," I said, and smiled at his confusion, then beckoned little Butterfly towards me and took a slender object from her hand. "You see this object, penis-head? Little more than a slim shard of our iron-wood, you see? Yet look how sharp and fine its point is…"

"Ye expect a man who's faced French cannon, guns and swords to quake in the face o' such a trifle?" he sneered.

I answered with—just a little—relish:

"In a moment, when I give the signal, some of these very angry and—you'll notice—quite strong gentlemen of ours will force you to your knees before my idol. Now, you know you can't prevent that. And then they'll drag you by the hair and maul you as they need until your face is grazed and torn and bloodied by the worn stone relict of my vagina. And when they do that, you will kiss it."

"Never, bitch!"

"Did I omit, by the way, to mention, that when they've bowed you before me, this slender spike here in my hand will be introduced to the opening of your anus?" I saw something different in his eyes now—something I wanted very much to see.

"What!"

"If they are compelled to bow you by force, Cacopardo, this half yard of very rigid, very sharp timber, will be placed at the opening of your arse. If you then resist, and for so long as you resist, this lovely little girl here, will feed it into you, little-finger-breadth by little-finger-breadth—and just look at her tiny little fingers, what d'you say; a quarter inch—a quarter inch at a time?

So very sharp it is, you see, both pointed and keen bladed—indeed those of ours who shave their faces would happily use this for that purpose—and on my command, scarce a quarter inch at a time, she will begin to push it, ever so slowly, through your innards, prodding, slicing. I'm sure the pain will be quite exquisite."

Remaining defiant, forced to his knees, it took less than a half inch to convince him and he fell on the stone cunny like a man much in love.

Being seen to do so by his comrades seemed to break him and for their part the others needed no convincing, though the weak-kneed one was allowed to bestow no more than his tears, so far gone was he in terror, and shortly thereafter we arrived at the punishment ground.

But four pegs already seated in the earth, we stood by as Tandi fetched a handful more from the cavern, and waited whilst some of our men hammered them hard into the ground. As soon this was accomplished, each prisoner was toppled, one man at a time, and stretched spread-eagled twixt the wooden pegs, each peg serving for one hand or ankle of two men. Never, I think, in the island's history, had so many felons been thus punished at once and we were briefly concerned that we might not have the apparatus. We did, though, and swift enough there were five prostrate men with their cocks encased in the sealed and readied moulds, held firm in place by our warriors.

I could not, though, mix enough of the compound for all at once, having just the one bowl for the mixing and another for hand washing, and no one else was permitted to do this duty, so I was thus compelled to attend to them one at a time. One consequence, of course, was to protract the business, but our people were not in any hurry.

Cacopardo nearest, I began furthest away with the youngest of the crew. Tandi carrying and holding the bowl of mixture, Butterfly maintained the second bowl, constantly emptying it onto the ground and refreshing it with water from gourds supplied by other assistants. As I slopped the mixture in and firmed it down

I would rinse my hands very often, and always in clean water, so that not the slightest of the mix or contents might adhere to me.

Depositing the slop within the mould always provoked a pathetic reaction, as the cool and gluey mixture seeped around their naked cocks and balls, slowly building up around their unwilling erection. And we did not bother with the pissing tube. We knew they would scarce live long enough to require it.

I was mixing the second bowl when the first felon began to moan, was inserting the first handfuls into the second mould when he began to cry, and by the time the second was filled, burying the blind eye of an otherwise quite attractive cock forever, the first man was screaming like a little girl and writhing—so much as the restraining guards would let him—in a most pathetic agony.

Not knowing what was happening, all but Cacopardo had turned their heads to stare. They could not know, and the cool mix could never at first portend, that the alchemy of the mix was such that it heated as it hardened, searing and blistering at the last, and the youth was feeling his cock and balls cooking slowly like a hedgehog in gypsy clay. I had felt but a shadow of that burning many years before when I first practiced the art, despite my frequent hand-washing, and I did not envy them now.

The first had passed out in pain and terror ere the second man began to cry out, and as I tended the third I heard the second pleading with his God for some relief. Unsurprisingly, it came not.

I think my concentration upon the task perhaps relieved me of some of the emotion which their crying and pleading might have otherwise induced, but in truth I felt quite pitiless, as cold and hard as the watching faces of the crowd, as the stone when it finally set.

The priest, the last, was sorely discomposed, though he tried not to show it, alarmed at his vulnerable nakedness as much, perhaps, as the anguish of his crew. He asked me why they were screaming so, and I answered not a word, just slopped the mixture in atop his lice.

The stones were set by morning and the men gazed in red-eyed horror at the shell-and-pebble-studded cannon balls that the moulds, removed, revealed. They were startled then to be cut free and distraught when they sought to move, weighed now to the ground by the concretion in which balls and cock and curling hair were one, the slightest pull on which brought agony to their unseen blistered skin.

Men dragged them to their feet and our convicts needed no bidding or instruction but found themselves, quite naturally, with both hands around their dragging weights.

It was then we marched them to the pool below the cliff, their greatest discomfort arising as they slithered down the steep and slippery rocky bank, jarring, scraping and bruising their feet on stones, inadvertent jostling of ball in groin making them whimper in pain.

People now began to move away, confident of the outcome and ready to return to living, and the felons watched them go, a look of comic perplexity on most of their faces. Because it was my task I took a seat atop the bank, my legs splayed, cunny exposed, my new slave sitting beside me obedient as a spaniel, and Summer, Tandi and Butterfly near. The king stayed too, the council, and but a handful of the guards.

Seeing us so few and finding themselves but instep-deep in pleasant tropic water, the captives essayed a try or two to clamber up the bank. Cacopardo, to be fair, did not even try, merely gazed on me with a passion of hatred which I suppose was intended to discomfit me. It did not. Only as the day wore on did I become, in my heart, a little sorrowful, gazing upon these men so practically imprisoned by their balls as so many others are in metaphor, whilst watching the water rising up upon their naked helplessness.

Their terror knew no bounds as the water rose from instep to calf, from calf to knee, from knee to groin, then over their hands and over the stones, then lapped about their navels, crawling slowly upward from rib to rib, to sternum, neck and chin, then over till it came as a terrifying kiss upon the ridge of the lower lip. The first and shortest among them flailing in a sudden panic forgot the weight around his balls and sank with a sudden scream. The four who remained dragged themselves through the imprisoning water toward the pool-sides, tried to position themselves higher on the bank, but the endeavour was entirely useless and only prolonged their final threshing and their dying. Then it was done.

We never moved the bodies, just noticed from time to time how they diminished, and speculated, I suppose, on how in their solid accretions their pricks would be the last to be eaten by the myriad small beasts of the drowning pool.

All our invaders' possessions deep-buried or burned, there soon remained no reminder of them save those who were yet sadly missed and the dark, quite comely youth who slept beneath my roof.

Waited upon already to such an extent that it was almost more than I could endure, it is perhaps not to be wondered at that I had little idea of what to do with a slave, save what my loins first thought of. He proved, in the end though, a very real treasure.

In the immediate aftermath of the invasion of our island there were, of course, the funerals to attend to, our people favouring immolation upon a pyre high up in the mountain whence spirits float up with the smoke toward the waiting moon.

The main ceremony, happily for me, only required my presence and was conducted by Gorrogo and a young male acolyte of his own. Of those who were grieving—which, in effect, meant most of the village—most on the day simply embraced me, each of the women gently and briefly kissing my teats, the breasts of the Mother Moon providing succour—in their faith—to the dead upon their journey to her womb.

Afterwards, in privacy, some few of those most suffering came to worship her in me and seek our blessing.

I was, besides, again the hero of the hour, having interposed my most symbolic moons between the whip and Summer's ever-lovely curves and having, as the king explained in loving, minute detail, composed and helped to execute the plan which had rid us of the penis-headed pig.

Being both grateful to me and impressed at my divine prowess there was, in consequence, a lovely surfeit of villagers all eager to receive whatever blessing, bestow whatever gifts and kindnesses, their newly-gentled hearts could think of. Both the captains of our warriors and a number of their men were eager to renew themselves by imbibing at my founts, and I was very pleased to let them.

I had named my new slave Jonah, in part ironically for having brought his companions so little fortune but principally in honour of the whale between his legs. Not at all unprepossessing, and not only in his truncheon, he beamed an almost constant smile in the joy of his reprieve, and I was loath to have him bound—as I must—at times when inattention and the perfidy we still suspected might lie within his heart, might have allowed him to escape and perhaps to cause us mischief. I doubt, now, that he would have, but there was then no way of knowing, and he was quite submissive to the deed, not even subjecting me to the merest look of reproach.

My girls bound him, for whatever reason, twixt two of the house wall's posts so that he stood or sat always with his back to the wall, and he was standing thus, his arms apart, for much of the time a silent witness to my cunny's ministrations.

Not surprisingly, therefore, there were times when I could not but help noticing that what he witnessed stirred him, and that the engorgement which that produced did most befit his naming. I coveted that whale at once, desired most desperately to entrap it and feel it spume within the sea-wet net that lay within me, yet knew not how to bring it about. I remembered a little pantomime, of course, later confirmed in words and in the wonderful acts of marriage, which had demonstrated that I could indeed have a cock within me, but not a man's seed. I wondered how much more such restrictions might apply to him, since he was not, after all, one of us.

My older girls, though, saw his lusting, and by now they well knew mine, and as soon as they were sure he was sufficiently tame they happily prepared him for me.

I returned from a brief excursion to find him strapped upon the bench, mystified yet smiling, his prodigious member swelling to the teasing of my Summer, little Butterfly teasing his lips with her slit, and as I entered the room Summer produced the gossamer-thin sheath, drew it over him and tied its cords beneath his balls.

Tandi, to her apparent joy, had 'drawn the short straw' in this enterprise, and Butterfly standing aside, Tandi stood her long slender body over him, eased herself down, and covered his face with her mound, they having decided between them that it was not appropriate for him to see the pleasure he might give me. The long, slim wand of her body, arse-cheeks small as my own still pert breasts, began to rise and fall gently upon him like a small boat riding a gentle swell, her own face soon sinking forward and her long hair falling a curtain before her. I could see her cheeks clench, sense her sphincter tighten, watch her back arch, as she rode the lovely surf of his probing tongue, could hear her moaning softly with delight.

And watching thus, feeling the echoing moisture warming in my loins, sensing the silken lid slide softly open, feeling the surge in the little pink eye of I and the prickling of the little hairs around the gently engorging pads of my lips, I lowered myself easily onto him. So big, so hugely filling, stretching the under mouth of me as if the lips might tear, the muscles within me clenching, grasping at him, drawing at him, pulling him deep and in.

He filled me so. He touched me everywhere. I slid him and rode him, feeling the cock-like skin of the sheath upon the yard that was hard as wood and yet so very different, flexing and giving, stroking me, caressing me, soft in my wetness, hard where it touched some divine inner peak of me.

And Butterfly, so aptly named, so tiny and so slender, then sat so softly upon him too, the cheeks of her buttocks caressing those of sweet Tandi, and she leaning forward, her face a soft question, her hand slid forward towards me. 'Oh yes!' and her hand was there, too, the tiny intelligent finger finding and touching, caressing and blessing my own little clit.

Did I scream, then? Was that me? That shuddering, juddering, that vibration was mine, that rippled so warmly, and the sweet hurt of a bent-backward back that's hard-arching was mine, and the warm ache around her was mine, and I had felt him in his coming, had felt that sweet pulsing, no matter that it was contained.

The both of us came, and Tandi was sagging, drunkenly slewing, subtly intoxicated by warm wetness of tongue, and I slid myself from him, took the sheath from him, swallowed him liquidly whole as he softened, clung to the sweet little bud he became.

It was a beginning, and he quietly charming, his life tied to mine now he cared for us all, took his part in the cooking, his part in the cleaning, his part in the cleansing of each with fresh sponges.

My acolytes, like myself, were not permitted to know penetration for so long as they might serve me, unless 'twas penetration with a toy or sheathed member. When they left me, as Summer, as June and some others had done, their lives were immediately restored as their own, their cunnies, their hearts, wombs and minds their own again, and all mine now—save Butterfly and Tandi—had had their children and their men and their man-hoods melting in them. How much I wished, sometimes, for that.

But how could it be?

"I was reminded by my wife," a quiet Arshon one day told me, "of an old story she thought you might favour."

I nodded, comfortable on a pile of furs and naked, enjoying the hospitality of his home, Minnarra glancing up at me and smiling. He said:

"Our history tells us that long, long ago, the god of fire descended from the sun to live among our people just as you do. It was he first made sticks burn, showed our people fire's making, and gave them the gifts of night warmth, light and of cooking." Arshon smiled: "The story says he lived with us some years, was loved and admired and was worshipped, that he served us a very long time. Only then he fell in love with a girl of the island, but knew he could not have her. He was a god, you see—the god of fire—and had he entered her she would have been consumed.

"The wanting that he knew began to age him, and often he was seen to weep, his tears becoming steam as they issued from his eyes, and the people—who loved him—knew this was not good, and prayed to their other gods for guidance.

"After many weeks of fruitless prayer they realised their folly, for what was he after all except a god and equal to any that they prayed to? There was nought he could not do. And because he had acolytes as you do, gentle followers well trained in his way, the people made a proposal which he accepted.

"In a ceremony that they say was very, very special, a celebration that went on and on for days, the fire-god passed his gift to a chosen student, gave the power of his godliness to him. In consequence the acolyte became the god, the god became a mortal and high priest, wedded his love within a moon and lived thereafter a loved and respected man, till age and mortality claimed him.

"And his gift, as you can plainly see, stayed with us—we still can make fire, after all."

"One day," I told him gently in English; "my lord may understand how very much I love him."

And so it became.

The ceremony lasted two exhausting weeks, its culmination something I will never, ever forget.

The final event was not perhaps so unusual, I'd cunny-loved each of my girls over time and often several of them at once. This time however what we did would take place in the open, in the centre of the green, before the thrones.

I had spent my whole life upon the island naked and had thought myself a long way past ever minding it, but never in my life felt I so vulnerable as the day I was carried to the couch where Butterfly waited, both of us watched with great anticipation by every adult in the village.

The couch was quite large—it had to be—and conducted thence, bowing to our King and Queen, Butterfly had then lain down upon it. Not bowing—for I was a god—I knelt astride the small girl's face, looking towards her feet, along her body, and carefully lowered myself toward her lips. A drum beat sounded as her tongue touched me, another as I leaned down, another as I placed my face between her thighs, another as I kissed her there.

A steady rolling beat now began, echoing the heart and pulse beat of our two oiled and painted bodies now conjoined, and a slicking and licking, that soft gentle probing, faster and faster, our people all watching, then suddenly—we were rolling.

Butterfly atop me I heard the crowd sighing and in me I was sighing and weeping and crying for joy at my freedom, for joy at her tonguing, so sweet and so gentle, so loving and kind. And now she was gushing and arching, fast-tonguing and my face was so wet with the wetness of her, and my loins were hard pushing and suddenly—I cried. I cried aloud, not theatrically, not for the benefit of a marriage audience, but for the first time for myself, as a woman does in joy.

And Butterfly was lifting and so gently turning, her belly and breasts were nuzzling mine, and her mouth was at my mouth lips and her tongue was within me and we were embracing and wholly in love and blind to the crowd's loud applauding.

Butterfly rose, first kneeling, then standing above me, looking down at me in public as never she could, for she was the god now and I but her priestess, and I took my god's hand and I rose to embrace her and bowed, now a woman, to my king.

Epilogue

We live, still, together, so much that you'd think little changed. Only at my insistence it is I alone who bathes her, who wipes her and tends to small intimate needs. And at night we're together quite often, though she has her Tandi and a new girl to love her.

Butterfly now, though, sits on the love throne, is tongued by the supplicants, is imbibed from by warriors who afterwards may still come to me. No god, now, but priestess, I still have the power, no god, now, but priestess, I now have the choice.

And I have two men, too, and I am requited.

I have felt the great whale of my Jonah blowing and wet in my net, felt it surge, rush and thrust, known contentment, and I still have my girls. If you could but see us as we are, sometimes, my Jonah within me as I lie spread-eagled, my big toes and fingers each in their own cunny and another to taste, if I wish it, or his cock in my mouth and the false-cock within me, my darlings still giving and taking such pleasure.

So very great a joy. But I do have, too, another man, the owner of the cock from which I so often supped in the small and dark pavilion of the Moon. And I know now why my girls stayed so quiet, and I know why they were timid.

Minnarra smiled:

"I know you love him, just as I do—I know he loves you, just as I do, and it is quite done for the king to have a concubine."

I gazed on her, bewildered. She continued:

"Knew you not that it was him in the Temple of the Moon, that it was him, my love, that you supped from?"

"I came to know, but I did not understand. I thought it part of the ceremony."

"It was a gift," she answered smiling; "a gift to him and to you from me."

Sometimes I share their bed, now, and my tongue knows her

as she once knew me, and she is wondrous.

"You know I am not—was not—a god?" I asked him once. He smiled dryly.

"Were you not?"

"You know, don't you?"

He laughed a little laugh:

"What do I know? I know that you are human, that you were human when you came from out the sea. I did not know that straight away but my sisters Sum-mah and Joo-oon soon did so."

"Then why did you not stop it all?"

"Stop what, Me Lady?"

"The lying…"

"I heard no lies. You did as you were asked to do and did it well. Perhaps you were not a goddess, after all, but that did not mean that the gods had not sent you—you who were so strange and, yes, so very beautiful."

"But when the blessings did not work!"

"There were some small disappointments, yes, but people learn to live with those, and who asks anything of a god with certainty of an answer? You brought us luck. We had the son we wanted, others did too, and other prayers were answered. You were kind to those who needed it, gentle and supporting, you made my people happy and," he smiled; "provided endless inspiration to my warriors. How do you know it was but mortal doing, that if not a god you were not at least gods-sent? What do you really know of the powers of that treasure you keep so warmly buried in that garden?"

What could I answer?

The ship arrived in my eighteenth year by island count, bristling with cannon, alive with curious men and officered by that strange blue-coated breed, confident as gods, wise to the winds and tides, steering impossible tracks by the guidance of the stars.

We saw it coming. There's a stockade around the village now, built after the raiders came and made at my suggestion to help avoid another such horror, and a watchtower on it surveys the sea and beach. At the first alarm I climbed up into the watchtower and felt a strange leap in the pit of my belly at the sight of the familiar flag, the sleek wooden, sail-billowing manifestation of famous might and power.

In consequence I met them on the beach, clad myself in a dress and petticoats long out of date and feeling very strange indeed, the king coerced into the fine knee breeches and a shirt, a group of others wrapped around with the fabrics from my bales. The Pilgrim Fathers themselves would scarce have flinched at the sight of us.

A longboat brought their Captain ashore with an officer and several men, the Captain the very model of a man in his blue and white and gold.

"Captain Brunty, ma'am," he introduced himself; "commanding His Majesty's Ship 'Convention' —a French ship, ma'am, till we took her."

I'm sure she enjoyed being taken by you, I thought, but introduced the king instead, then myself by my old married name and title. That seemed to startle him:

"Odd's fish, milady, but I knew your late husband well when we were last out here on station. A very fine gentleman, indeed."

My late husband? "I beg your pardon, Captain, but did you just refer to my 'late husband'?"

He could not have been more apologetic:

"Demmed sorry, milady, truly, never thought, but of course you could not know. I fear he died amid an outbreak of the cholera, back in eighteen-five."

"Back in eighteen-five? Pray, sir, and forgive me for being so out of touch, but I fear I do not know the present year."

"The Year of Our Lord Eighteen Hundred and Seven, milady."

I learned, thus, that I was widowed and an heiress, that they had come in search of certain piratical characters, including one

Padre Cacopardo for whom—at least—they'd arrived several years too late, and that England was at war again with France. I learned something else as well.

However admirable some of them might be I could see things in their faces, in their eyes and their expressions that I knew at heart I'd never see in the faces grown so dear to me, and, my gods, I could smell them too, and must fight to keep my nose unwrinkled. It was not the hard decision I'd expected.

I apologised on the king's behalf for the paucity of our hospitality, explaining that our village was currently subject to a plague to which just a few of us had proved immune. He was welcome, we told him, to forage on the land and to take water, but it would be best and safest if he kept his distance. And he agreed, sailors ever wary of diseases that can rake a ship from stem to stern in the time it takes to cough, happily accepting our offered hospitality and volunteering to take any letters or packages I would care to send and see them forwarded to England, marking us on his chart as a place to call for supplies.

So it has remained. The plague proves most disconcertingly persistent, despite the luxuries that the disposal of my assets in England has provided, and still the ships call from time to time, even a French frigate toward the end of the war, and leave us in peace, themselves replete with the freshest of fruit and water.

I'm past the energetic time of life, now, though Jonah and I do more than cuddle on most nights, and my girls are grown into mature women, and their girls also. My children, Summer and Tommy, grow strong, fine and intelligent, and at night we sit naked by our fires, look up towards the stars and thank the Mother Moon that we were never cast away upon that cold wet island, England, I now remember only as a dream.

R V Raiment was born and educated in Yorkshire,
Northern England, and now lives in Surrey.

With many thanks to those many friends at ERWA,
without whom this story might never have been written,
and in gratitude to Elspeth and Huw at Velluminous Press
for the enthusiasm, support and hard work which have
brought this book to reality.

Lightning Source UK Ltd.
Milton Keynes UK
19 January 2011

165974UK00001B/36/A